HER PERFECT HERO

A heartwarming, feel-good romance to fall in love with

EMMA BENNET

Originally published as *I Need a Hero*

Revised edition 2022
Joffe Books, London
www.joffebooks.com

First published in Great Britain in 2015 as *I Need a Hero*

This paperback edition was first published
in Great Britain in 2022

Cover art by The Brewster Project

ISBN: 978-1-80405-535-9

This book is dedicated to all the lovely ladies at the Aberhonddu Angels WI in thanks for all their support and many fun evenings!

CHAPTER ONE

At the end of a little lane just over half a mile from the town of Nettle Wood in Kent, there are two adjoining cottages. One stands empty and abandoned. It has no name. The other, Blackberry Cottage, so titled because of the abundant blackberry bushes at the bottom of its back garden, is clearly well loved. Its small front garden is beautifully tended, even in the leaf wreathed grip of early autumn. Wild rambling roses grow up a bower over the red front door with its polished brass knocker. Bright curtains hang from the windows, and through one an enormous black cat stares out at the world. This cottage is the home of thirty-year-old Bronte Huntington, a writer of romance and firm believer that her Prince Charming will be around very soon to sweep her off her feet. He's just been held up for a while.

Inside her home, Bronte is collecting together her latest work ready to present to her fortnightly writing group. She's running late, having got caught up finishing off a tricky scene. She lets down her long brown hair from her work-time bun. No time for full make-up, but her clear skin doesn't need it; her face is almost line free. She puts on just lipstick and a touch of mascara. A spritz of perfume, her scarf and hat to protect her against the nippy evening air, and she's

1

ready and on her way. Little does she know that in the few hours she's gone, something very exciting will be happening next door.

* * *

Bronte smiled as her friends called out a welcome to her from the corner they'd managed to commandeer for their meeting. The White Swan, the rather old-fashioned pub they met in, wasn't busy, but they usually liked to tuck themselves away as much as possible, none of them were exhibitionists when it came to giving readings and discussing their work. The group were known and respected by their fellow patrons, who did their best to leave them in peace, only listening in if something exceptionally gripping was read aloud by a particularly favoured author.

Bronte looked forward to these gatherings. Living pretty out of the way, and working from home, she'd often go days at a time without seeing anyone if she didn't make the effort to go down to the town.

The writers were a diverse lot, most of their offerings were far more literary than Bronte's romances, but that didn't seem to bother any of the other members, who looked forward to the regular instalments of her popular Scottish Highlands series, with its lairds of the manor and various damsels in distress being rescued, always within Bronte's allotted word limit.

Once she'd bought herself a white wine, Bronte settled down on a bench next to her best friend, Camille, a tiny, slim French woman with jet black shoulder-length hair, who wrote murder mysteries under the pen name Jack Sniper. Camille's novels were extremely bloodthirsty, and Bronte made sure she never read them when she was alone and it was dark outside.

As the last few stragglers hurried in, they started the meeting proper. They began, as always, by going around the table so anyone could share any news. Bronte had performed the rather dispiriting task of deleting over five thousand words from her latest manuscript and was much commiserated with. Next, those who wanted could share their latest work with the group, who'd do their best to offer some constructive criticism. More often than not, this was begun by the lovely Norman, a man closer to eighty than seventy, who'd self-published his memoirs of life as a long-distance lorry driver. Upon retirement, he'd discovered that he and his wife, Doreen, didn't actually have very much in common, and writing was his escape from the constant DIY projects Doreen had ready for him and the threat of OAP coach trips to the coast. It was because of dear Norman that a rule enforcing fifteen minutes of reading time maximum per author had needed to be introduced.

The official meeting ended at nine, but a few of the younger members stayed behind for a final drink, so Bronte didn't make it back to Blackberry Cottage until after ten.

Camille drove her home, and it was she who pointed out the lights on in the empty cottage attached to Bronte's own.

"Do you want me to hang around and check everything's ok?" Camille asked. "It could be burglars. Or a murderer, escaped from prison and searching for his next victim!" she added half-jokingly, allowing her writer's imagination to get the better of her.

"I don't think a burglar or a murderer would turn quite so many lights on, especially as it's obvious my house is lived in," replied Bronte, sounding braver than she felt.

Getting out of the car, along with Camille, who was adamant she wasn't leaving her friend alone until they knew just what was going on, Bronte stood at the twin gates, still debating what to do. The matter was taken out of her hands, however, when the chipped front door to the unnamed cottage opened. A voice called out, "Hello there!" and a figure made its way along the dark path.

The stranger was male, and just an inch or so taller than Bronte in her heeled boots, making him about five foot six. He was so bundled up in layer upon layer of clothes that it was quite impossible to tell what his physique might be like beneath it all. His face was open and friendly, and peeping out from under the woolly hat he wore pulled down low over his ears, was bright ginger, could-be-related-to-a-Weasley hair.

"Is one of you Bronte?" he asked with a strong Irish lilt as he got to the gate and looked expectantly at both women in turn.

"I am," replied Bronte, with one hand in her bag trying to locate her personal attack alarm, though she appreciated it was rather unlikely he planned to do her any harm, especially as he knew her name.

"Great, I'm Ryan Murphy. My Aunt Joanna owns this cottage and told me about you. I'm a dentist and I've just started work at the practice in town. My aunt said I could stay here until I got myself settled."

"Oh! Well it's very nice to meet you," said Bronte with a smile. She'd only met the wonderfully bohemian Joanna once, when she'd come to pick up some stuff she'd stored in her cottage, not long after Bronte had moved to the area. They'd discussed herbaceous borders and poetry over a cup of tea, and that had been the last Bronte had seen of her kaftan clad neighbour. It would be good to have next door occupied, it looked so sad and lonely sat there next to her own far cheerier home.

"Let us know if there's anything we can do to help you get settled," piped up her friend, her usually light French accent thickening seductively in unconscious reflex at meeting a new man, "I'm Camille."

Ryan took her outstretched hand.

"Bronte's usually about, she works from home. Just knock on her door, anytime! I'm sure she'd always be pleased to see you," continued Camille pointedly.

"Yes, thank you, Camille. Let's get inside, it's cold and Ryan must have plenty to be getting on with. I'm sure he doesn't want to stay out here chatting to us all night," said Bronte, alarmed that her friend seemed to have got it into her head to try to set her up with her new neighbour.

Saying a swift good night, Bronte ushered Camille into her cottage, almost tripping over the cat on the way in.

"Be careful, Mr Darcy!" exclaimed Bronte, picking up her pet, "Did you miss me?"

The cat's angry hiss and scramble to get out of his owner's arms suggested he had not in fact missed her company. His ensuing stomp to the kitchen to meow by his bowl revealed the real reason he'd left his spot next to the warm wood-burning stove to greet his mistress.

Bronte gave him his food and attempted to scratch him behind his ears as he came to eat. He moved deftly out of the away, flicking his tail crossly.

"You know," observed Camille, "It wouldn't surprise me if that animal had deliberately positioned itself to trip you up as you came in."

"Don't be silly," said Bronte, putting the kettle on.

"It seems to hate you," said Camille, eyeing Mr Darcy suspiciously.

"He's just aloof, like his namesake."

Keeping watch on the cat, Camille took the tea Bronte handed her and, moving enough of her friend's scribblings out of the way so there was room to put her cup down, sat at the large oak kitchen table.

"So . . . What did you think of Ryan?" Camille asked with a twinkle in her eye.

"He seemed nice. Friendly. He didn't mention anyone else coming to join him, so hopefully it'll just be him and he won't be too noisy," Bronte said noncommittally.

"Yes, yes, but what did you think of him? He's quite scrummy isn't he?"

"If you find small, bundled up red-headed Irishmen attractive . . ."

"Oh come on! He was cute!"

Ignoring her friend's comment, Bronte continued, "And he's a dentist! Have you ever heard of a less sexy profession?"

"Undertaker," replied Camille instantly. "Undertaker would be less sexy than dentist. Just imagine what you could get up to in his chair!" she winked.

"I hate going to the dentist and I especially hate getting in the chair," said Bronte grumpily.

"Won't you even consider him? You haven't been out on a date for ages."

"Ryan Murphy is most definitely not my type," Bronte said with finality.

"By which you mean he isn't one of your fantasy lairds, or actually Jane Eyre's Mr Rochester himself," said Camille with exasperation.

"There's nothing wrong with having standards."

"There is, if it means you won't give a decent man a chance," muttered Camille into her cup.

* * *

The cottages had once been one large four-bedroom house, but at some point in the distant past the then owner had seen fit to put in a dividing wall and create the twin two-bedroom homes. They were certainly on the small side, but full of character. Bronte had fallen in love with her quirky little place the moment she'd pulled her car up outside for a viewing.

The walls separating the two cottages were thin and Bronte was so used to next door being empty that it was strange to hear the early morning noises as Ryan moved around and got ready to leave for the surgery. She heard him start his car and drive off as she was settling down at the kitchen table to begin writing. Bronte found she needed to be quite strict with herself and stick to a proper timetable otherwise the day just seemed to get away from her. It took a lot of discipline to work productively from home with a demanding cat and the internet to distract her.

* * *

Bronte heard Ryan arrive back in the evening. She even heard him switch on his kettle a moment later, and the ting of spoon against mug as he gave his drink a stir. For someone used to the total silence of living alone, practically in the middle of nowhere, it was strange and rather distracting.

It was a chilly but beautiful evening, so Bronte abandoned work at six, and went outside with a novel and a cup of coffee. Sitting herself down at her little cast-iron table in the shade of the ancient plum tree, denuded now of all its gorgeous fruit, she wrapped a tartan blanket around herself and opened her book, ready to lose herself in the story. She was re-reading an old favourite, Jane Austen's Persuasion, and Louisa Musgrove was about to make her infamous leap from the steps at Lyme Regis. Mr Darcy deigning to join her, even though he settled well out of reach, glaring, completed Bronte's feeling of contentment.

She'd only read a page or two when she was drawn from her book by a cheerful call of "Hello there!" Looking up, she saw Ryan's smiling face peeping over the top of the fence dividing their land. The original garden had been cut in two like the house, resulting in two long, but rather thin, plots.

"Good evening," replied Bronte, not wanting to appear rude, but anxious to return to her book.

"I was wondering if you had a minute to help me. I haven't quite got the hang of the wood burner in here yet. Would you mind showing me what I'm doing wrong?"

"Of course not," said Bronte, putting down Persuasion with a small inward sigh.

Ryan's cottage was certainly cold, it was no wonder he'd been so well wrapped up the night before. Bronte came in the front door, which led directly into the sitting room. It smelt a little musty, like it needed a good airing after being shut up for so long. Several cardboard boxes were rather precariously stacked against one of the walls. There was a small sofa still covered with a dust sheet, and a large very comfortable-looking armchair. A book lay open on it and further volumes were piled on the floor next to the chair, along with a couple of mugs with coffee dregs in the bottom. Crouching down in front of the offending wood burner, Bronte began poking around, rearranging the logs. Out of the corner of her eye, she saw Ryan removing the mugs.

"There's a certain art to getting these going," she commented. "Have you got some newspaper?"

"Sure, there's some upstairs."

Ryan brought them down, and before long Bronte had a decent fire going.

"Thank you so much. You're a handy woman to know."

"No problem, they can be a bit tricky if you're not used to them. I take it you weren't in the Scouts."

"I'm afraid not," said Ryan with a laugh.

"Well, I'll see you around," said Bronte, turning to go.

"I was just about to open a bottle of wine, if you'd like to stay for a drink?"

Bronte debated: she was keen to get back to her book, but Ryan seemed nice and it would be good to chat to someone after working by herself all day. Plus he was going to be her neighbour; it made sense to get to know him a little. And she didn't want to be thought standoffish.

"Sure, that would be lovely," she said, smiling.

The door to the kitchen was closed, presumably to keep in any heat. Leading the way, Ryan opened it and a waft of warmth and spice hit Bronte, "Wow, that smells amazing," she commented.

"I made some chilli, would you like some? There's masses and it'll be ready soon."

"OK . . . yes, thanks," said Bronte tentatively. The food did smell very good, but she wasn't quite sure how she'd gone from reading by herself just a few minutes before, to spending the evening with this virtual stranger.

"Have a seat," said Ryan, pouring them both a glass of wine. "Please forgive the mess. I had to go into the surgery today so haven't had time to get things sorted."

Open boxes littered the floor, he'd clearly just unpacked what he'd needed to cook with.

"I'm hoping to get everything sorted at the weekend," he continued, "But I'm a bit at a loss as to where I should start. The cottage hasn't been lived in for so long, it needs a good clean and a bit of fresh air."

"I can give you a hand if you like," Bronte found herself saying. Where had that come from? She didn't even know this guy!

"That would be brilliant, if you're certain you don't mind?"

"Not at all."

Ryan cleared the small Formica table. The two matching chairs were the only seating in the room.

"Apologies for the state of the furniture, I don't think anything has been updated in this place since the seventies."

He served up the chilli with white fluffy rice, yoghurt and salad. He's certainly a good cook, Bronte thought as she tucked in.

"I hope it's not too hot for you. I tend to make my chilli pretty spicy."

"It's great," said Bronte. She took a large swig of wine to cool her mouth.

"So what do you think of Nettle Wood so far?" she asked.

"The little I've seen of it seems great. Compared to the tiny village I hail from, Nettle Wood is a heaving metropolis."

"So you're a bit of a country lad are you?"

"Well I went to university in Dublin so I'm not a total bumpkin, but pretty close to it."

When they'd finished eating, Ryan made them both a coffee and they moved back into the sitting room, now considerably warmer thanks to Bronte's earlier efforts. He rather nobly insisted she take the armchair while he perched on the edge of the covered sofa.

"You like Dickens," commented Bronte, picking up the book which lay on the floor by her feet. "I love Great Expectations, too."

"Yes, I've lost count of the number of times I've read it."

The pair soon became caught up in an intense discussion regarding the respective virtues of their favourite books. Their tastes often differed, but this only served to make the conversation lively. It came as no surprise either to discover that they'd both been in debating club at school. At last, Bronte checked her watch and was shocked to see it was almost eleven.

"I'd better be going," she said with a sigh. "It's getting late and Mr Darcy hasn't been fed, he'll be in a foul mood with me."

"Mr Darcy?"

"My cat," said Bronte, blushing. "He's rather temperamental and doesn't like waiting for his tea. He's liable to attack my ankles when he sees me now."

"Shall I walk you home and protect you?" asked Ryan gallantly.

"I think I'll be OK, but thanks for the offer!"

He held the front door open for Bronte. "It's been a great evening," he said, stopping her.

"Yes, it has."

"I was wondering if I could take you out for dinner sometime."

"You mean like a date," she said with surprise.

"Yes."

"Oh, Ryan, thank you for asking, but I don't date."

"You don't date?"

"Nope."

"Can I ask why?"

The wine she'd drunk encouraged Bronte to answer this more honestly than perhaps she would have had she been stone-cold sober.

"I think it comes from writing romances for a living. It's made me very aware of exactly what I want in a man, and I'm afraid I haven't yet met a man in real life who quite lives up to the fantasies I create. No offence."

"None taken. I can appreciate that a dentist living in a cottage full of seventies furniture might not cut it compared to, say, Heathcliff?" Ryan said, hazarding a guess.

"Well, he was a bit nuts, but yes. So until that man arrives, my hero, the one who takes my breath away and changes my life forever, I'm not dating."

"Fair enough," Ryan said, looking just a little bemused.

"But I'm happy to come and help you at the weekend, if you still want me to? I'd like to be friends."

"Friends it is then." He shook her hand firmly as she left.

Bronte walked down the garden path. Turning into her own gate, she looked over her shoulder, caught Ryan's eye and received a last smile. She was glad she'd explained herself and he hadn't been hurt. It would be horrible to have any sort of awkwardness between them.

Bronte dodged Mr Darcy's ready claws as she served him his belated dinner. As she climbed into bed that night, she thought about the lovely evening she'd had with her new friend.

CHAPTER TWO

Bronte was up bright and early on Saturday morning, carefully planning her outfit. It needed to be practical enough to clean and move furniture in, but she didn't want to look a total mess in front of her new neighbour. She opted for a wholesome, land-girl, dungarees-and-checked-shirt look, tying a scarf around her hair to complete the ensemble.

She fed Mr Darcy and went to knock on Ryan's door.

"It's open," he called from somewhere upstairs.

His house already felt more like a home. It was warm for a start. Ryan had managed to keep the wood burner going, and the smell of fresh coffee hung in the air, mixed with the faint tang of woodsmoke.

"I'll be down in a minute! Help yourself to a drink!"

Bronte followed the heavenly scent to a full cafetiere in the kitchen. She poured herself a cup of coffee and turned to find Ryan standing in the doorway. He must have rushed out of the shower: damp patches mottled his t-shirt, and he self-consciously ran his hands through his still wet hair.

Bronte's face reddened at the thought that he'd probably been naked a moment ago when she'd arrived. She felt like a teenager coming face to face with her high-school crush. "Sorry, am I too early?" she muttered awkwardly.

"No, not at all, thanks for coming," he said. He came over and gave her a welcoming hug before helping himself to a coffee. He smelled fresh and citrusy, and Bronte couldn't resist taking a deep sniff.

"Where do you want to start?" she asked, deliberately attempting to clear her mind of unclothed images of him.

"Maybe upstairs? That way the dust will fall down?"

"Sure."

"I've got supplies," Ryan indicated to the table, which was covered in cleaning products, cans of white paint, rollers and paint trays.

"The paint's for the main bedroom," he explained. "Flower power's gone crazy up there."

Laughing, Bronte followed Ryan up the stairs, doing her best to concentrate on the things she was carrying rather than watching his bottom ahead of her. What was the matter with her? she thought crossly.

He hadn't been exaggerating about the state of the wallpaper in his bedroom, it was like stepping into a psychedelic time warp. But Bronte found his unmade bed much more of a distraction. He seemed a little embarrassed by the sodden towel and discarded clothes strewn on the floor that he hadn't thought to clear up before inviting Bronte upstairs.

"Sorry," he muttered and put the offending items in the washing basket.

"Don't worry," Bronte laughed. Then, determined to bring things back to what she'd come for, she added, "We'd better get this wallpaper off. Have you got enough dust sheets?"

"I thought we could use those curtains, they're going straight in the bin anyway. I bought some blinds to replace them with," Ryan said, pointing to a long cardboard package in the corner.

Easy conversation, picking up from the evening before, eventually lapsed into companionable silence, with the radio blasting out to keep them motivated. It wasn't a large room and the wallpaper was old: it came off without trouble so it wasn't long before one wall was ready to be painted. Bronte wielded the roller while Ryan started stripping the next section. Occasionally he seemed to forget she was there and sang along with a song on the radio. She failed miserably to hide her smiles. When he absentmindedly began busting a move, she could hold onto her giggles no longer.

Hearing her despite the music, Ryan turned around, blushing, before swiftly deciding to get his own back. With a wicked grin on his face, he grabbed a roller loaded with paint and advanced slowly, threatening her with it. "You think my dancing's funny, do you?" He held the roller mere centimetres from her nose.

"No, no!" screamed Bronte, laughing. "Not at all!"

"I don't think I believe you!" He moved it closer still.

"Have mercy!"

Ryan relaxed his grip. Quick as a flash, Bronte snatched it from him and rollered his hair. "Sucker," she declared triumphantly.

Ryan looked shocked, "I can't believe you just did that," he exclaimed, searching around for a way to exact his revenge.

"Truce!" Bronte shouted desperately.

"And why do you think I'll agree to that?"

Bronte was suddenly extremely aware that Ryan was very, very near to her. She felt hot and her stomach started doing somersaults.

"Because if you do, I'll make some tea and get you some of the shortbread I baked yesterday."

"Hmmm . . . Truce accepted," he said solemnly.

Before he could change his mind, Bronte ran down the stairs laughing. She put the kettle on and went to retrieve the biscuits.

* * *

Around one, they stopped for some cheese-and-pickle sandwiches and ate them at a rather rickety table and chairs set up in Ryan's garden. The wind rustled the drifts of dry, fallen leaves and the weak autumn sun warmed Bronte's face as she raised it to catch the light.

They chatted about books again mostly, bickering when they disagreed about a particular author's merits, with pleasantries resuming when they reached agreement. It was so comfortable being with him that it was only when Bronte went to use the bathroom that she spotted quite how much paint she was covered in. She rubbed off what she could and made herself presentable. Staring at herself in the mirror, she realised she looked really happy. Yes, her hair was still a bit of a mess, and her clothes were paint-splattered, but her cheeks were pink from the fresh air and her eyes gleamed.

Going outside again, she said, "I can't believe you didn't tell me I was covered in paint."

Ryan shrugged. "I thought you looked kind of cute."

"Oh," replied Bronte, unable to prevent a little smile from breaking out.

After washing up their lunch things, they cleaned the bathroom and gave the second bedroom a good clear out: grouting was scrubbed, mould patches painted over, taps polished, windows were washed, beds moved, and carpets vacuumed. They were both small rooms, but it was hard work, and they got through a lot of bleach in the bathroom in particular. By the time they finished for the night, they were both exhausted, but the upstairs was gleaming.

Ryan insisted upon treating them both to a takeaway and a nice bottle of wine to thank Bronte for all her help. He went out to pick up the food while Bronte ran next door to feed Mr Darcy and change out of her paint-mottled clothes. The cat eyed her disdainfully, suspecting he was going to be abandoned again, as she fussed over him and dashed around in her underwear looking for a clean outfit. Back at Ryan's, she found glasses, plates and cutlery for them both. She also gave the sofa a good hoover and flung a blanket over it, which at least made it safe to sit on.

When Ryan returned they ate in the sitting room with the food on their laps and watched television together, eschewing the usual Saturday night fodder, relieved that neither of them liked it, and chose a Miss Marple marathon instead. They both swore to take the knowledge of the other's rather old-fashioned taste to the grave.

At some point they must have nodded off because when Bronte woke she was leaning against Ryan, who was fast asleep. Checking her watch, she saw it was after midnight. She got up, her neck aching, and considered waking Ryan as well so he could go up to bed, but he looked so comfortable she didn't like to disturb him. Instead, she covered him with a blanket and left a note next to him saying, "See you, tomorrow sleepyhead." Then she quietly snuck out of the door, locking it behind her and posting the keys back through the letterbox. She narrowly avoided tripping over Mr Darcy, and was in her own bed and back asleep within ten minutes.

* * *

The following morning, Bronte was a little later going round to Ryan's cottage and knocked on his front door wearing her fall-back 'stylish decorator' outfit of faded jeans and layered tops, and with her hair in two plaits.

"Are you absolutely sure you don't mind helping me again?" he checked, "I wouldn't want to take advantage of your good nature."

"Positively certain!" said Bronte cheerfully. "It's lovely to see the old place being sorted out. I moved into my house three years ago, and the estate agent said no one had lived in either of them for ages."

"Yep, Aunt Joanna bought her cottage years and years ago. She planned to use it as a country escape, but it turns out she loves the city, and never wants to come down here. The whole family's been telling her to sell it for years, but I'm glad she didn't now."

Following Ryan into the kitchen, Bronte helped herself to a cup of tea from the pot brewing on the table. Ryan popped some bread in the toaster for them both and they planned what they were going to get done that day. Now that the upstairs was clean and looking a lot better, they'd focus on the sitting room and kitchen.

The big job was the kitchen so they started there. The house had been empty for so long that all the cupboards were filthy, festooned with dust and cobwebs. While Ryan washed windows and wiped down walls, Bronte cleaned out cupboards and the rather ancient fridge-freezer.

They stopped for a lunch of Cornish pasties, which Ryan had picked up from a local store and warmed up in the now gleaming Aga. They ate in the overgrown garden again, washing their food down with large mugs of tea, glad to be in the fresh air and away from the dust and the smell of cleaning products.

After their food, the pair reluctantly hauled themselves off the somewhat rusty garden furniture and headed back inside the house to tackle the sitting room.

It was handy that Ryan had so little stuff and also hadn't really unpacked: it meant it was a simple matter to move the furniture into the centre of the room, making what looked like a funeral pyre to bad taste.

The curtains were chucked and blinds put up, instantly updating the room. The dark hardwood floorboards looked pretty good after a good scrub and polish. The sofa and arm-chair were still in a bit of a state, but with some decent throws and cushions covering the orange polka dots, they were much more presentable. The wood burner also looked much better for a clean.

* * *

As the afternoon drew to a close, raindrops began to fall and pattered against the newly smear-free windows. The tired pair stood in the centre of the kitchen and took a good look at their work. The place really did look an awful lot nicer. Removing the old, faded net curtains allowed a lot more light in, and getting rid of the dust and opening the windows had made the air inside much fresher.

Ryan handed Bronte a coffee. "I'll unpack the rest of my cooking things and make us both some supper, if you'd like to stay."

"That'd be great, I'll give you a hand to get the stuff out."

Bronte peeked nosily into the cardboard boxes. "You don't have much."

"I've moved around a fair bit. Never really had a chance to hoard."

"How long do you think you'll stay here?"

"A while I hope," he replied. He held Bronte's gaze for just a second too long, his hand brushing hers as he also reached into the box.

"You might have to buy some more pans in that case," said Bronte, moving her hand and attempting to defuse the sudden electricity between them.

"Especially if I can get you to agree to dinner with me on a more regular basis," Ryan replied lightly.

Bronte didn't know how to respond. How had this happened? Had the playfulness gone too far and she'd somehow given Ryan the impression she was interested in him? Or was she reading too much into it? She thought she'd been very clear that she just wanted to be friends. Maybe she shouldn't have offered to help him — it might have given him the wrong idea. It was just so nice to have someone next door and she'd been happy to help make the little cottage look better. He was also very good company and she'd enjoyed getting to know him, but he absolutely wasn't hero material, and she hadn't meant to lead him on in any way! Bronte tried to push her thoughts to the back of her mind. She was overthinking things, as usual!

Ryan clearly wasn't so concerned about any awkward atmosphere. He was cheerfully humming along to the radio and peeling potatoes.

Bronte flattened down the empty cardboard boxes and moved them against the wall, before beginning to lay the table.

Going over to the cupboard next to the oven, she reached up to get a couple of glasses. Bringing them down, she turned and found herself face to face with Ryan. He was so close she could smell the fruity shampoo on his tousled hair and had an impulsive, rather disturbing urge to run her fingers through it. Surprising herself, she dropped the glasses and they smashed on the floor around her feet.

"Oh my goodness, I'm so sorry! How clumsy of me!" she jumped back and bumped into the oven, as much to move away from Ryan as the broken glass.

"Don't worry, it doesn't matter," he said softly.

Bronte fussed around getting a dustpan and brush. Bending down to sweep up the mess, she stopped suddenly when Ryan put his hand on hers. She looked up into his eyes and the desire to kiss him washed over her: torn between moving towards him so she could give into it and just running away, Bronte stayed stock still, crouched on the kitchen floor. As if sensing her confusion, Ryan brought his hand up to stroke her cheek.

This second touch shocked her into action. She couldn't let this go any further. How had she even allowed things to get so far?

Getting briskly to her feet, she backed away from him, her mind whirring as she tried to work out how to get herself out of this situation, and fast.

"I'm afraid I really must go," she blurted out.

"Go? But, Bronte . . ."

"I'm sorry," she said, opening the front door to let herself out. "It's my cat you see . . ."

"Your cat?" repeated Ryan.

"Yes, my cat, Mr Darcy. I must, erm, feed him. He can't wait. So sorry."

And with that she rushed out of the house and into the rain-filled evening.

CHAPTER THREE

Bronte marched down Ryan's garden path and out of the open gate. She didn't go home. Despite the horrible weather, she felt the need to walk, and to get far away from the terribly awkward situation she'd found herself in.

Crossing the dense verge, she plunged through tall grasses, bramble, and the dying-back remains of the summer's willowherb and cow-parsley, the wet stems drenching her jeans. She slipped into the woods, hoping to find some shelter from the building rain. But the relentless flurry of light drops only became replaced by heavier gushes as the water splattered down through the trees, and in a matter of moments Bronte was soaked through. She wished she'd had the forethought to at least grab her coat before storming out.

What on earth had happened in Ryan's kitchen? She couldn't really blame him. She knew she was as much at fault as he was, if not more. She'd encouraged the playfulness and the flirty banter as they worked, but he was a dentist for goodness sake! Who'd ever heard of any woman lusting after a dentist? How long before he started talking dentures and wisdom-tooth extraction? This clearly wasn't a man she could contemplate spending the rest of her life with.

After Dean, she'd sworn she'd never waste any more time on men who clearly weren't right for her. It was three years ago now, when she'd lived in London, but it felt like a lifetime. Deep down, she'd always known that it would never work out, but somehow she'd kept on deluding herself, always hoping, and making-do. And in the end, after thirty wasted months, he'd decided she wasn't quite right for him after all. She'd thought he was going to propose when he took her to the restaurant and she had got dressed up especially in a 'getting-engaged outfit' she'd picked out weeks before. She'd waited patiently through the first two courses, wondering if he'd already bought a ring and, if so, how he was going to present it to her. Would he ask her on bended knee in front of the whole restaurant? Or wait until they were walking home, just the two of them? It was a gorgeous moonlit night, perhaps he'd suggest they have a walk down by the Thames, taking in some of the sights of the South Bank, and he'd propose there. Perhaps he'd ask her on the London Eye . . .

When they'd first started dating, Bronte's friends had all warned her about Dean. He was a renowned womaniser, lead guitarist of a band who'd had great things predicted for them when they first got together, but several years on had failed to reach anything like those dizzying heights. Spending his days working as a session musician, Dean was still sure his band would make it big, and his enthusiasm and confidence were pretty irresistible.

What had started off as a bit of fun became more serious when Dean's landlord decided to sell the house he shared with the rest of the band, and Dean moved in with Bronte. She ignored the voice in her head telling her he was only living with her because he couldn't afford anywhere else. Her friends were amazed by how she'd managed to 'tame' him, but she maintained that "when a man finds the right woman, he's ready to settle down."

A year later, and Dean's band broke up. One of the members was moving away and it had become clear to everyone, with the exception of Dean it seemed, that the group was going nowhere.

Dean took the news better than Bronte had thought he would, even accepting a job at an insurance company to give him a steadier income than his session gigs.

Then, about two months before breaking up with her, Dean began coming home late from work and acting rather distant. Bronte worried he was having an affair, but when she confronted him, he was just so smooth and plausible: he was doing overtime for their future, and sure, he might have been a little off recently, but that was only because he was exhausted working so many hours — all for them — and she was letting her writer's imagination run away with her. He looked so hurt by her accusation and sounded so convincing. Of course, it was all lies, and she really should have trusted her instincts.

Eventually, he'd said he wanted to talk to her about something, and, somehow, she'd managed to convince herself that all the overtime was so he could buy her an engagement ring and save for a wedding. The slight hesitancy through it all, the quiet note of discomfort, could simply be explained away by pre-popping-the-question nerves.

The setting was lovely, a gorgeous bistro on a little backstreet. Dean waited until she'd put the final mouthful of her crème brulée into her mouth before telling her he thought they should see other people, and that, actually, he had been, for quite a while. Then he left, leaving her to pay the bill.

Once the initial devastation had subsided, her prevailing emotion had been anger. Anger that she'd allowed herself to be duped. If she'd just listened to her head, or practically anyone else for that matter, she never would have wasted so much time with a man who was clearly never going to commit to her.

After that, one evening when she'd had a little too much to drink and was feeling sorrier for herself than she liked to admit, she made a vow. A vow never to waste another minute on an unsuitable man. She got rid of anything that reminded her of her ex (quite an expensive exercise it turned out) and she moved out of their flat in London and into her beloved cottage. Her vow served as a reminder of what she was looking for in a man, as did her novels, in which she allowed her imagination to run wild creating the heroes she longed for in real life. She would never again settle for a man who was less than perfect.

She believed that someday she would meet her 'one.'

* * *

Bronte liked walking and often found an hour rambling around the woods helped clear her head. It had solved many a tricky plot problem in the past. But she didn't usually set off in this direction and it wasn't too long before she broke off her musings and realised she was completely lost.

Trying to think clearly, and remember everything she'd ever heard you ought to do if you find yourself lost in the countryside, Bronte assessed the situation: she had no phone with her, no torch, no map, not even a compass — not that she was confident she'd have known what to do with it even if she did have one. She wasn't sure where she'd come from and seemed to have been wandering in circles. Either that or there were a lot of identical fallen trees around here. With the light rapidly falling, she knew she needed to come up with a plan, and quickly.

Deciding she'd be better able to work out where she was if she could see more, and knowing the woods couldn't actually be as large as they seemed at the moment, Bronte walked in as straight a line as possible, figuring she'd eventually come to the edge of the wood.

She focussed firmly on putting one foot in front of the other and not stepping in anything too muddy, doing her best to ignore any strange rustlings and hoots around her. Her calves began to ache as the ground became steeper.

When, with a huge sigh of relief, she finally emerged from the trees and found herself in more open countryside, she realised she must actually have been climbing steadily for longer than she thought: she was now at the top of a hill, in the distance she could make out the lights of the town.

Thank goodness, she thought to herself, pleased she'd been able to find her way out by herself. If she just worked her way slowly down, she could warm up in Camille's house, and she was sure her friend would give her a lift home. She'd sneak into her cottage without Ryan seeing her and work out what to say to him tomorrow.

Unfortunately, she'd somewhat underestimated quite how steep and slippery this side of the hill was. She'd descended about a quarter of the way when she lost her footing. She gasped as she fell painfully on her ankle.

Rolling over and over through the mud, her hair was pulled and her face scratched as she crashed over twigs and nettles. Finally, she came to a stop thanks to a large patch of brambles. She was soaking wet, filthy and hurt.

The town and its lights could still be made out, just as distant. Blinking back tears, she gingerly attempted to stand, but her right ankle gave away immediately, the sharp, swift pain making her cry out. Everywhere ached, but nothing else seemed to be seriously damaged, thank goodness. What was she going to do? There was no way she could get home by herself in this state, and no one knew where she was. She didn't even have her mobile phone with her to call for help.

The landscape seemed far darker and far more sinister than it had earlier. Any sensible thoughts about what she should do left her, and she began to panic and screamed out frantically, "Help! Help! Can someone please help me?!"

She shouted until her throat was hoarse, then finally, faintly, she heard something: the sound of a horse's hooves coming closer, and then a deep male voice calling, "Is someone there?"

"Yes! Yes! I'm over here!" Bronte replied, relief flooding through her.

From out of the shadows and gloom, an ominous, misshapen figure approached. Strange and amorphous, it lurched nearer . . . then resolved into a horse and rider, making their way gingerly down the muddy slope.

Her rescuer jumped off his steed and knelt beside her. As he came close enough for her to be able to see something of his features, for a moment all her pain and discomfort was forgotten. He was tall and strapping with wavy black hair. He wouldn't have looked out of place on a catalogue photoshoot. What caught her attention most were his dark eyes with their long, dark eyelashes. Her heart skipped a beat.

"Are you alright?" he said.

"No, not really!"

"What's your name?"

"Bronte."

"I'm Sebastian. Can you tell me where it hurts?" he asked, remaining reassuringly calm.

"Everywhere!" Bronte sniffed and tried to stem her tears, which had begun to flow freely, partly from pain, partly from the great relief of being found.

A sympathetic smile broke out across the man's face. He took off his coat and placed it around her shoulders.

"Can you tell me anywhere it hurts in particular?"

"My ankle. I fell on it."

"Can you walk?"

"I don't think so, I can't even stand up."

"You're very lucky I came along when I did: usually I would've been back home ages ago. Put your arms around my neck."

"Excuse me!"

"So I can help you up."

"Oh, thank you," said Bronte with embarrassment.

She sat herself up and, as instructed, put her arms around his neck. He lifted her up gently. She was acutely aware of what a state she was in, but her overwhelming feeling was one of surprise at just how easily he was managing to carry her.

Before she could protest, she found herself on the back of the horse. She squealed as the animal took a small step forward, worried it would either slip on the mud or gallop off, leaving her clinging onto its reins for dear life.

"It's alright," her saviour said, showing her he had hold of the bridle.

He leapt up behind her in the saddle, taking up the reins with his right hand and putting his left arm around Bronte to hold her steady. She tensed up immediately, jarring her sore ankle and making her wince.

"Would you like me to take you to the hospital?" he asked.

"No, thank you. I don't think anything's broken, I just need to get warm."

"Then, may I give you a ride home?"

"Would you be able to drop me at my friend's house? She lives in the town."

"Of course."

Bronte gave directions as best she could, and leant back against Sebastian. She was exhausted and frozen, but nonetheless quite enjoying the experience of being properly rescued for the first time in her life.

Arriving at Camille's house, Bronte's knight in shining armour swung himself off the horse, landing elegantly on the ground, then lifted Bronte down and carried her effortlessly up the stone steps.

"Oh my goodness! What happened to you?" exclaimed Camille when she came to the door.

"An altercation with a hill," Sebastian answered for Bronte. Her teeth were now chattering despite all her efforts to still them. "May I bring her inside?"

"Of course!" Camille stood aside, seeming distinctly impressed by Sebastian carrying Bronte over her threshold and into the sitting room, where he placed her gently down on a sofa.

"Is there anything else I can do for you?" he asked Bronte.

"No. Thank you so much for rescuing me," she said, "If it hadn't been for you, who knows how long I would have been stuck out there."

"I'll leave you with your very capable friend then. It was a pleasure," he replied, smiling. He turned to Camille, "Please contact me at the Fenworth Estate if Bronte needs anything. I'll see myself out."

Camille looked as if she were dying to question Bronte about her handsome rescuer, but seeing the state she was in, decided against it for the moment.

Camille helped her up the stairs and managed to get Bronte into a piping hot bath. She poured her a large whiskey, for medicinal purposes, and left her to soak and warm up. Once Bronte had thoroughly defrosted, her friend brought through some dry clothes.

Camille suggested Bronte stay the night but, worried about Mr Darcy and wanting to be in her own bed, Bronte declined. Camille gave Bronte a hand into her battered old Renault Clio and took advantage of the short drive to quiz Bronte on her mystery man.

"How do you know him? How come you haven't mentioned him before? I imagine he meets all your criteria for hero material!"

"I don't know him. I'd never seen him before he turned up on the hillside and rescued me."

"And he was seriously riding a horse when he found you?"

"Yep, it was just like when Marianne meets Willoughby in Sense and Sensibility."

"Didn't he turn out to be a bit of a scoundrel?" asked her friend absentmindedly as she slowed, indicated and turned into the narrow lane leading up to the two cottages.

"That's beside the point," said Bronte haughtily.

The car came to a stop in front of Bronte's house. Ryan was presumably still awake, as his downstairs lights were on.

"Turn off your headlights," hissed Bronte, slipping down in her seat so she was below the car window.

"What are you doing?" asked Camille.

"I don't want Ryan to see me."

"Whyever not?"

"I just don't. Please turn the lights off."

"OK, whatever you want. I hope your night vision is up to scratch."

The headlamps went off and Bronte gave her eyes a few seconds to adjust to the dark.

"I'll come in and make you comfy," said Camille.

"If you could just give me a hand inside, I'll be alright," whispered Bronte, opening the car door.

She twisted round in the seat. Camille was still fussing around, getting out of her side of the car. Wanting to be as quick as possible to avoid being caught sneaking back home by Ryan, Bronte heaved herself to her feet. Pleased she'd managed to stand, she attempted to step forward, but in the darkness mistook where the rise to her front gate began and stumbled slightly, putting her weight on her weak ankle.

"Ow!" she cried, grabbing hold of the car door to steady herself. Camille hurried over to her. At the same time, Ryan appeared in his doorway and called out, "Is everything alright out there? Is that you, Bronte?"

"Yes, it's me. I'm fine thanks," Bronte said through gritted teeth.

Ryan disappeared from view but returned to the door again a moment later with a large torch. He quickly came over, shining the light on them.

Not giving her friend a chance to turn down much needed aid, Camille piped up with, "Ryan! How lovely to see you again. Actually, things aren't fine at all: Bronte's had a bit of an accident. She's hurt her ankle. Do you think you could give me a hand getting her inside?"

"No problem," he replied. "What happened?" he asked Bronte, looking concerned as he put an arm around her. "Lean on me."

"I fell in the woods."

"It's not a very good idea to go running off into the woods just as it's getting dark," Ryan said pointedly. "How did you find her?" he asked Camille.

"I didn't."

"I was rescued," said Bronte simply.

"By whom?"

"By Sebastian."

"Just Sebastian?"

"He didn't tell me his surname. He was a little busy saving my life!" Bronte replied dramatically.

"Fair enough," muttered Ryan.

"He was tall with dark hair and gorgeous hazel eyes . . . He was riding a big horse."

"He said we could contact him at the Fenworth Estate," Camille added.

"Sounds like you met The Honourable Sebastian Fairfax, son of Lord Fairfax," Ryan said.

"The Honourable?" repeated Bronte.

"My aunt knows the family a little. From what I hear, he's just the sort to be riding around the countryside in the rain picking up damsels in distress."

"He's the son of a lord?!" Camille squealed.

"Yep. His father owns the Fenworth Estate."

"Yikes," exclaimed Bronte.

They all went inside Bronte's cottage. Ryan made Bronte a cup of tea while Camille got her settled on the sofa.

"Will you be alright by yourself tonight?" Camille asked. "Are you sure you don't want me to take you to Accident and Emergency to get that ankle checked out?"

"If it's still really sore tomorrow, I'll go to see the doctor. You get home, it's late."

"OK, I'll call you in the morning," Camille bent down to give her friend a hug. "Ryan, I'm off!" she called into the kitchen.

"Do you want to borrow my torch?" He came back into the sitting room with Bronte's tea.

"Thanks, we don't want anyone else injuring themselves in the dark tonight."

Camille left and Ryan gave Bronte her cup of tea. He sat down next to her on the edge of the sofa, "Right, let me take a look at that ankle of yours."

"It's fine," Bronte pulled it away, wincing as she moved.

"It's not fine, and I've done first-aid training," he replied firmly.

Bronte gave in and gingerly rolled up the leg of her trousers. Kneeling beside her, he very gently examined her injury.

Bronte felt awkward, and attempted to break the tension by quipping, "I'm glad I shaved my legs this morning."

Ryan smiled, "So am I."

He pronounced the ankle, "sprained and bruised, but not broken," and insisted upon strapping it up for her.

He popped back home briefly for his first-aid kit and gave her some painkillers before bandaging the ankle. Bronte did have to admit it felt a lot better.

After some protest, she even agreed to let him help her up the stairs to her bedroom. He closed the window and brought her a glass of water while she brushed her teeth and struggled to get into her pyjamas in the bathroom.

"I'll get going," he said, once he'd ensured her leg was elevated, and she was completely comfortable and had everything she needed.

"Thanks for all your help tonight."

"What are neighbours for, eh?"

There was a moment of self-conscious silence.

"I'm sorry about running out on you earlier."

"It's not a problem."

"No, it was rude of me."

"I made you uncomfortable." He looked down at his feet, clearly ill-at-ease. "It won't happen again."

"I'd really like it if we could still be friends."

"So would I."

He bent down and kissed her on the cheek. "Goodnight. I'll pop by to check on you in the morning."

Once he'd left, and with the knowledge and relief that they were friends again, Bronte's mind was free to wander back to Sebastian. She went over every delicious detail of their meeting until she finally fell asleep.

CHAPTER FOUR

Bronte was up and hobbling around early the following morning. The night had passed painfully and fitfully, so once her clock said seven, she thankfully dragged herself out from the tousled sheets and slowly hopped about. Her ankle, though terribly swollen and still very painful, definitely felt better than it had the night before.

At eight thirty, Ryan knocked at her door and Bronte invited him in, gratefully accepting his offer to make tea and toast — after he'd checked her ankle. The bruising was coming out in some beautiful shades of purple, but he could see she could move it more and was able to put greater weight on it, so agreed with her that it was improving.

He'd begrudgingly been reassured that she really didn't need to see a doctor, and was about to leave, when there was another knock. Ryan automatically answered it for her, saving Bronte from getting up.

"Hello?"

"Good morning. I'm looking for Bronte Huntington, have I got the right house?"

Bronte heard the conversation and her heart lifted when she realised who it was: Sebastian. So, he was interested enough to find out my surname and my address, she thought to herself happily.

"Yes, she lives here," replied Ryan stiffly, "But she's not able to come to the door."

"Are you her husband?"

"No. A friend."

"Well, I just wanted to check how she was. I'm Sebastian Fairfax, I found Bronte last night."

"I'll let her know you came by," said Ryan, clearly doing his best to get rid of her visitor as quickly as possible.

Before he could actually slam the door in Sebastian's face, Bronte called out, "Sebastian! How kind of you, please come in."

Her gentleman caller strode into the house in search of her. He was so tall that he had to stoop to get through the low kitchen doorway, unlike Ryan, who was able to enter with space to spare. Sebastian carried a huge bunch of beautiful, deep crimson roses which he gallantly presented to Bronte.

"Oh wow! They're gorgeous. Thank you," she said. "Would you like a cup of tea or coffee?" She ignored Ryan's scowling face.

Making himself comfortable at the table, Sebastian replied, "A tea would be lovely, thank you."

"Would you mind putting the kettle on?" Bronte asked Ryan, gesturing at her ankle.

"Not at all."

"Oh, and could you please get me down a vase, while you're on your feet?"

Ryan silently, and a touch sullenly, thought Bronte, made the tea and fetched the vase, while she and Sebastian chatted away about her injury.

Mr Darcy sauntered into the room and headed straight for Ryan. Purring, he rubbed against Ryan's trousers. Then he stopped and stood stock still: he had spotted Sebastian. With his eyes fixed on the strange man, the cat's tail went absolutely straight then, with a horrifying yowl, he suddenly leapt at Sebastian's outstretched leg.

Sebastian let out a shocked squeal, springing to his feet almost as quickly as Mr Darcy had pounced. He began a mesmerising one-legged dance, obviously in pain, straining to shake off the hissing lump of black fur while avoiding putting his hands near it. Ryan looked on, head to one side, thoroughly amused judging by the smile flickering on his lips.

Bronte shouted, "Mr Darcy, no!" and struggled to get up and help. Before she'd actually made it to her feet, Ryan belatedly darted in and scooped up Mr Darcy, more out of concern for the cat than poor Sebastian, she thought. As soon as he was safely in Ryan's arms the animal calmed down and even began to purr, though his eyes remained steadfastly fixed on the ruffled Sebastian.

"Shall I put him outside?" Ryan asked.

"Thanks, that might be a good idea," said Bronte gratefully. She turned to Sebastian, "I really am so sorry, I don't know what got into him. Are you OK? Did he draw blood?"

"It's fine." Sebastian checked his leg for claw damage.

"Don't you need to go to work?" Bronte asked Ryan, noticing the time.

"Yeah," said Ryan, putting Mr Darcy down by the open back door. The cat ran out, hissing as he went, his tail upright. "I'll come and check up on you again this evening, shall I?"

"Thanks, see you later," Bronte replied perfunctorily. She turned back to Sebastian to give him her full attention.

"I'll let myself out," Ryan mumbled to himself as he left.

Sebastian stayed for an hour, then left to deal with 'estate matters.' He'd been very attentive, and kept going over how lucky it was that he'd found Bronte when he had, "I dread to think what could have happened," he'd said with a shudder, taking Bronte's hand in his. "It must have been fate, we were meant to come together."

Bronte was very flattered; their conversation felt like something out of one of her own novels.

"Just imagine what a story it will make to tell our grandchildren," he'd continued with a little wink.

Bronte had tried to focus on her teacup in an effort to steady herself. They'd really only just met, yet her gut was telling her he was what she'd been waiting for, and amazingly he seemed to feel the same way she did. He was so handsome and chivalrous, he made her feel special. She could hardly believe her luck.

As he was going, he'd said, "I'd love to see you again, if I may? Take you out on a proper date. When your ankle's up to it, of course."

"That would be lovely," Bronte had gushed, tilting her face a little towards his in case he'd wanted to kiss her goodbye. He didn't, but that had only slightly dented her euphoria.

Her head full of Sebastian, Bronte arranged the roses and then read until lunchtime when Camille arrived.

Her friend immediately noticed the beautiful flowers.

"From Sebastian I take it?" she asked, grinning broadly.

"How did you know?"

"He was at my house this morning wanting to know how you were and where you lived. He was quite delightfully anxious about you. I'm very jealous."

"He's very charming and he appears to like me, but there's no guarantee I'll see him again," Bronte said, trying to convince herself as much as her friend, so she didn't get too overexcited.

"I wouldn't be so sure, he seemed pretty keen when I spoke to him. Did he just leave the flowers or did he hang around?"

"He stayed for about an hour and said he'd see me soon."

"What did I tell you? But what about the lovely Ryan?"

"There's nothing going on between me and Ryan."

"Maybe not, but he'd certainly like there to be."

"He knows the score. He's not my type," Bronte said firmly.

"Kind, thoughtful, good job, great looking, intelligent . . . all adds up to not your type?"

"If you think he's so amazing, why don't you ask him out?"

Bronte regretted her words as soon as they were out of her mouth. She suddenly felt uneasy.

"I would if I thought he was the slightest bit interested in me," said Camille.

"Kind, thoughtful, good job, great looking, intelligent . . . these add up to make you not his type?" Bronte teased.

"I suspect at the moment his type is just you."

"If you're right, and I'm not saying I think you are, then he'll soon get over it. I really just want us to be friends."

"OK, I believe you. What do you want for lunch? I'll rustle us up something to save you hobbling around on that poor ankle, but don't expect anything too fancy, you know an omelette is about my limit."

"An omelette would be lovely."

* * *

After Camille left, Bronte got out her laptop. She planned to work on her latest novel, which she was about two thirds of the way through, but instead opened up a new document. A brilliant plot idea had just formed itself in her mind and she needed to get it down straight away. She automatically based her hero on Sebastian, and he seemed to come to life immediately. She called him Angus: he was strong, handsome and completely charming; she just knew her readers would love him. She suspected he'd be her most popular hero yet.

She worked on her new story until it got dark outside. She was so engrossed in her writing that she was surprised when Ryan arrived as he'd said he would. He was very kind, but could see that she was busy so didn't stay long, extracting a promise that she'd call him if she needed help making dinner. Before he went, he said, "Oh, I almost forgot, just a second." He dashed off and was soon back wielding a walking stick.

"I thought you might find this useful. I found it in the shed."

"Um, thank you," said Bronte, not wanting to appear rude, but grimacing as it was handed over. It was absolutely hideous: the wood was orange-coloured pine and extremely scuffed, with several chunks knocked out of it. Worst of all, the top was carved into the shape of a duck's head. The duck wore a rather natty top hat and bowtie, and appeared to be smoking a cigar, the tip of which had broken off.

"Sorry it's not much to look at, but you won't need it for long."

"It's really . . . nice . . . of you. I'm sure it will be a big help."

After he left, Bronte swiftly hid the walking stick in her broom cupboard, but immediately felt guilty. Ryan would expect to see her using it, and she didn't want to hurt his feelings — he was so considerate and caring. She took it back out and walked around the kitchen. OK, so she had to confess that he was right. Again. It did make things a lot easier, but she hoped she didn't have to resort to taking it anywhere she'd be seen with it!

* * *

Bronte finally put away her laptop at nine, closing the lid with a satisfied sigh. She'd made really good progress on her new story, with plenty of descriptions of her breeches-wearing Sebastian-inspired hero galloping across the countryside on his noble steed. She would have happily carried on, but Mr Darcy jumped on her keyboard, demanding attention.

Bronte attempted to pick the cat up for a cuddle but received a hiss and a clawed swipe at her hand in response.

She hobbled slowly into the sitting room, and settled down on the sofa with a book and the two thickest blankets she could find, not because she was particularly cold, but to protect her legs from Mr Darcy when he condescended to join her, his warmest cushion, and started his clawing to shape her for maximum comfort.

She heard Ryan moving about next door, and had an urge to see him. He really was very good company and so easy to chat to. He switched his television on and she wondered what he was watching. She smiled when she heard him laugh at something.

Whatever Ryan had been enjoying finished at half ten. Tired from the previous restless night, Bronte took this as her cue to turn in early. She swallowed a couple of painkillers, narrowly avoided tripping over Mr Darcy, and went up to bed.

* * *

Nine days later, and Bronte's ankle was much improved, though she still wasn't able to walk far or drive, pushing down on the accelerator in her ancient Mini was just too painful. She was desperate to get out of the house and Camille kindly picked her up and drove them to their writing group. Bronte caved and took the walking stick with her in case she had trouble getting around the pub, but planned to keep it hidden out of sight if possible.

The friends settled down with their drinks, meticulously wiping down the tables before placing any manuscripts on them. Bernard was halfway through his reading when a hush fell over the pub and at least three quarters of the patrons looked to the door. Bernard glanced eagerly up, clearly hoping his thrilling prose had caused the silence and that he finally had the attention he felt he deserved.

Bronte swivelled round to see what everyone was staring at. Sebastian Fairfax, as dashing as ever, was standing in the doorway searching the room. His eyes met Bronte's and he smiled. It was a second before it clicked that he was coming over to speak to her. Swiftly checking the hideous walking stick was well concealed under the table, she sat up straighter and smiled back.

"Just the woman I was looking for," said Sebastian when he reached the group. "I went to your home and when I found you weren't in, your neighbour graciously advised me where I'd be able to track you down."

Judging by Ryan's reaction the last time he'd encountered Sebastian, Bronte somehow doubted another meeting would have gone well. She stifled a giggle at the thought of Ryan's face as he opened his front door to find Sebastian on his step.

"Would you like to join us?" she asked.

"Can I get you a drink, sir?" offered Bernard deferentially. If he'd had a cap, it would have been doffed to within an inch of its life.

"Oh, no, thank you, I can't stay," replied Sebastian. Did Bronte detect a note of disdain in his manner as he glanced around the old, rather shabby building? She bristled at the thought: she was fond of the pub with its low-beamed ceiling and knickknacks covering the walls. Even if it was a little scruffy, she didn't like the idea of Sebastian sneering at it. But her concerns were quickly forgotten as Sebastian continued, "I just wanted to ask if you'd care to join me for supper tomorrow evening? I thought we might go to the restaurant at the Manor Hotel? It's rather good."

"Um, yes, that would be lovely!"

"I'll pick you up at eight, if that suits."

"Eight's fine," said Bronte happily, "I'll write down my contact details for you in case anything crops up." She hurriedly scribbled her email address and mobile and home phone numbers down on a scrap of paper torn from her writing pad. He looked at it as if mildly amused and handed her a thick, embossed business card in return.

"Till tomorrow," said Sebastian. Bending over, he took her hand and kissed the back of it.

Bronte's cheeks were bright red as she watched him stride out of the pub with his usual confidence and poise.

Naturally, all eyes were now on Bronte. The men managed to appear nonchalant, but the women were determined to have answers as to how she knew Lord Fairfax's son, why he was chasing her around town and, perhaps most importantly, what she was planning to wear the following evening.

Of course, the excitement built to even greater heights when Bronte regaled her friends with how they met and his chivalrous rescue.

Familiar as the tale was to Camille, she still got swept up in the girly, vicarious excitement. "I assume you're planning on using this in your next book?" she said.

"Oh yes," replied Bronte with a smile, "Actually, I've written a scene based on what happened. Would anyone like to hear it?"

There was a resounding "Yes!" so Bronte, still rather pink-cheeked, read through what she'd written. Bernard, knowing the spotlight had been lost, good-naturedly bowed out. By the end, all the women in the party were swooning and all the men humphing that "some men make it impossible for the rest of us!"

* * *

Bronte faced a small dilemma as she got ready for her date, what should she do about her walking stick? She'd already had to forego her beloved heels thanks to her stupid ankle. A walking stick would hardly give the impression she was hoping for.

In the end, she allowed vanity to win out, she was being picked up after all, so would only need to walk from the car into the restaurant.

She'd manage.

She was ready to go by eight, but it wasn't until quarter past that Sebastian drew up in a silver Aston Martin. He needlessly beeped his horn to let her know he was there. She limped unsteadily out to the car, her way illuminated by the headlights. She was sure she saw a curtain twitch at the front window of Ryan's cottage. Bronte's indignation that Sebastian was late and hadn't come to the door to fetch her was put aside once she saw the inside of his car and was treated to one of his most charming smiles.

"I thought we'd use the town car, take her for a bit of a spin," he said.

Radio 1 blasting out of the speakers made it hard to chat so Bronte amused herself by looking around the car's interior, taking in all the gleaming chrome and leather. She wasn't usually much of a car person, but this was something else.

Sebastian pulled away slowly, the engine a quiet rumble, apologetically mumbling that he was worried about the potholes in the lane, and that he'd "open her up" once they were on good tarmac. He was true to his word. Joining the main A-road, he pressed hard on the accelerator, opening the throttle. With a raucous snarl from the engine, gripping Bronte with a simultaneous shot of fear and excitement, they tore forward. Their speed too soon levelled out, the frisson diminishing along the straight with the uber-smooth flow of the car and the blur of the surreal, starkly illuminated hedgerows against the inky blackness, isolating her from her actual motion.

His erratic cornering broke the hypnotic spell and the fear returned along with the force pressing her back down against her seat on each corner. The exhilaration, the illicit thrill, didn't come back with it; this was outside of her comfort zone and Sebastian's driving was dangerous. He wasn't anywhere near as good as he thought he was, and they were going irresponsibly fast for this winding section of road with its sharp blind bends. Back on the straight, she braced herself against the dashboard. She was relieved when Sebastian, looking across, noticed her discomfort and slowed down, saving her from finding the non-ego-bruising interjection she was frantically searching for.

"Oh, I'm so sorry. Too fast for you?"

His tone was genuinely contrite, and his gentlemanly response mollified her right away. He's just trying to impress, she thought, and felt a little guilty with herself as the words 'fool' and 'show-off' lurked at the back of her mind for the remainder of the journey. Thankfully it didn't take much longer to reach the restaurant. Bronte was impressed with his choice: the restaurant was attached to a renowned country house hotel, she'd heard good things about the food and had been wanting to eat there for a while.

The restaurant was busy and lively, filled with a mixture of the hotel's guests and locals out for a treat. They were seated quickly in the large, high-ceilinged dining room. Sebastian ordered a bottle of champagne "to celebrate your ankle's recovery and our fortuitous meeting."

A log fire blazed away in the corner, making the room deliciously toasty. Its light glinted off the chandelier hanging in the centre of the room, casting mesmerising flickers across the walls.

"So, what have you been up to today?" Sebastian asked.

"Working mainly. I'm a writer."

"Your neighbour said you were at some sort of writers' meeting last night," he said as the scallops he'd ordered for them both arrived. Bronte would have actually preferred the goat's cheese salad, but hadn't liked to say. He'd seemed sure he knew what she'd enjoy.

"Yes, we get together every couple of weeks. We all write in different genres, but it's nice to have some feedback from other authors. I write romances, lots of dashing heroes and swooning heroines."

"What a fun hobby!"

Bronte couldn't help but be a little rattled by his comment, "It isn't a hobby, it's my career. I happen to sell rather a lot of my books!"

"Oh right! Well good for you!" Sebastian looked momentarily perplexed. "I think it's wonderful when a girl makes her own money, terribly um . . . empowering."

Bronte struggled to hide her shock — just what century was he from? But not wanting to ruin the evening with an argument, with a deep, calming breath she changed the subject, "How's everything with the estate?"

"So-so. The usual trouble with some unreliable tenants."

"It must be a huge responsibility."

"Well, yes, but I've been preparing my whole life for the duty of running it. It's been in my family for four centuries."

"How long have you been in charge for?"

41

"Oh, I'm still second-in-command, as it were. Daddy's training me up."

"Your father lives on the estate?"

"Yep, Mummy and Daddy."

Oh God, he still lives with his parents! thought Bronte. He must be in his early thirties! But then it's not like they're all squished into a two-bed terrace house, she'd seen their place, and it was huge! Perhaps they lived in a different wing or a cottage? But still . . .

"So what do you do at Fenworth?"

"Well, Daddy makes sure I sit in on the Monday meetings with the estate manager, and when the accountant comes . . . I ride the land a great deal, checking the fences are OK. Of course, the polo club takes up quite a bit of my time, you'll have to come and watch me in a match when the season restarts."

"That would be great."

"Do you play at all?"

"No . . . I'm afraid not."

Sebastian looked a little disappointed, so Bronte quickly added, "But what I've seen of it looks great fun."

This seemed to cheer him up, "We train a couple of times a week at least, during the season the actual matches are usually at the weekends. Actually, you missed an amazing practice on Sunday . . ."

Sebastian monologued about polo for the rest of their starter, all the main course, and only stopped for breath when the waiter brought them the dessert menu.

He really was very handsome, and it was like a dream come true for Bronte to have dinner with the son of a genuine lord, but she couldn't help thinking he was a tiny bit dull. And more than a tiny bit self-absorbed. He didn't seem interested in anything other than horses and polo! Neither was a subject she knew or cared much about, but that didn't deter him. It appeared of no consequence to him that she didn't contribute much to the conversation. She did her best to stifle her frequent yawns.

By the time Sebastian dropped her home, Bronte was almost relieved to be parting company with him. He walked her to the door, and kissed her firmly, dipping her down dramatically and completing the move with one of his charming grins. Bronte was left speechless.

"I'm going away for a week with the polo chaps, but I'll see you when I get back," were his parting words.

Letting herself into her house, Bronte couldn't help feeling a bit confused at how the date had panned out. She wasn't quite sure what she'd been expecting, but she certainly hadn't thought she'd be bored rigid for a large proportion of the evening! The car and the restaurant had been very impressive, and the kiss at the end like something out of an old Hollywood movie. It just seemed to be the company itself that was somewhat lacking.

* * *

Bronte awoke the next morning determined to be more positive about the previous night: maybe Sebastian had just been a bit nervous and that had made him talk about himself rather a lot. Perhaps if they went out again he might be more relaxed. She should have made more of an effort to steer the conversation towards mutual interests, but she'd been nervous herself, which couldn't have helped matters.

Was it also possible she'd built the whole thing up too much in her mind beforehand? She'd been waiting for her dream man to come along for years: now that it seemed he had, she was expecting everything to be absolutely perfect between them straight away. She needed to be more realistic: no matter how fantastic the guy, there was no getting away from the awkwardness of a first date. And surely that kiss made up for a lot!

She checked her email while waiting for the kettle to boil and was pleased to see Sebastian had sent her a message saying: *I had a marvellous time last night. Looking forward to doing it again soon, S.*

How many years had she spent writing about men like Sebastian, and wishing she could meet someone like him in real life? So what if their first date hadn't been perfect? The next one would be, she thought firmly. She was resolute that this was finally going to be her Happy Ever After.

CHAPTER FIVE

Bronte took some painkillers for her ankle, which was a little sore from the night before, and prepared to start work. She'd decided to abandon the romance she'd been writing in favour of her new tale. The old story wasn't inspiring her, and while it would be tough to meet her publisher's deadline starting afresh, she could do it if she focussed. She opened up the file containing the new book she'd been working on and began to write.

The charismatic hero, Angus, had invited her heroine, Pippa, to stay at his castle and they were stood in front of a fireplace. Bronte wanted them in deep conversation before being interrupted by someone. The problem was she just couldn't get the chatter between them to flow. She tried to get inside her hero's head, but all he seemed to want to talk about was polo and horses. Maybe she should have listened more to Sebastian the night before, at least then she'd have had something to sketch out.

Usually when she got a bit stuck she'd go for a walk, but her ankle definitely wasn't up to that this morning. She made herself another cup of tea and pottered around, putting on a load of washing and running the vacuum cleaner round.

She sat down again, determined to move her story forward. She added another description of her hero's dreamy brown eyes, based on the memory of Sebastian gazing across the restaurant table at her, but then found herself stumped again.

An hour later, she was still staring at the same spot. Not wanting to waste any more time, she eventually just typed, 'Hero is charming. Hero and heroine connect but interrupted'. She then moved on to Pippa exploring the castle, before stopping for lunch.

In general, Bronte was happy with this latest book: the setting was romantic, the heroine lovable, the hero irresistible, so what was wrong? Why wasn't it working? Why was Pippa so uninterested in what Angus had to offer? In theory, he was perfect!

* * *

Sebastian's week away passed quickly. Bronte left the new plot to mull around in her mind until she finished off the final edits of a short story she'd been working on.

She was typing away at her computer when she received a text from Sebastian saying he'd returned to Fenworth and asking if she was free to meet up soon. She texted straight back: *How about supper at mine tonight? 7 p.m.?*

Great! See you in a bit. S, came the response.

She checked the time and was surprised to see it was already past six. Oh blast! She'd lost track of the afternoon again. She was always doing this when she got absorbed in her writing. As well as a cleaner, she needed a PA too. OK, there wasn't any need for panic, but she'd better get a move on.

Although in a rush, she quickly realised the one thing she did have time for was to worry: she was concerned that the standard of her food might not be up to what Sebastian was used to. She really should have organised the dinner for another night, when she'd have been able to prepare more.

But he'd be getting ready now, and she couldn't very well cancel just minutes after inviting him. So OK, he probably ate restaurant quality food all the time, but surely he'd enjoy a cosy evening in her cottage, and her simple home cooking could be a nice change? It might even reinforce what a good wife she would make him one day!

Another stress was that Mr Darcy would have to be kept well out of the way. He'd taken an instant dislike to Sebastian when they'd met, and as ridiculous as it was, he wasn't a cat who readily changed his mind. She didn't want him attacking her date again! Maybe he could go to Ryan's while Sebastian was with her? But what if Sebastian stayed the night? She couldn't expect Ryan to keep Mr Darcy at his house until morning. No, she decided firmly, that was beside the point, she wasn't ready to sleep with Sebastian. And anyhow, she didn't like the idea of Sebastian staying over while Ryan was just one extremely thin wall away. How embarrassing would that be? It wasn't really fair to involve her friend in this at all. The cat would just have to be popped in the spare bedroom.

She shook off the thought of Sebastian in her bed and decided to focus on preparing for the evening ahead. She'd have to use whatever she already had in as her ankle wasn't up to walking or driving to the shops, not that she even had time to go out. She had a peek in the fridge and cupboards, but didn't find anything very inspiring. It was looking like supper might have to be Heinz tomato soup and cheese on toast! She'd wanted the evening to be relaxed, but maybe that was taking things a bit too far.

Finally, she found a packet of Arborio rice at the back of the shelf. Combined with an onion, stock, a large glass of white wine, frozen spinach and some roasted tomatoes, she could make a tasty risotto. She also discovered half a French stick which she'd use to make some garlic bread. That would be easy enough and give her a chance to sort herself out a bit.

She did the washing up and made the sitting room look nice. She just had a few minutes to change her top and brush her hair, when the doorbell rang. Bother! Well, on the plus side, at least he wasn't late this time, she sighed. Punctual would have been preferred to early, but the important thing was that he was here. Calling out, "Just a second!", she frantically shooed a grumpy-at-being-disturbed Mr Darcy upstairs and into his allotted prison.

She went downstairs into the hallway and opened the front door with her biggest, most welcoming smile, and found Ryan standing there.

"Ryan! Hi!" she said, catching her breath.

"Hey, are you alright?"

"Yeah of course!"

"Are you busy? I was hoping you'd come over and share a pizza with me, maybe stay for a film?"

"I'd love to, but Sebastian's due any moment. We're having supper together."

"Oh right, no worries then, some other time. Um, I'll get going."

"See you soon?" said Bronte, feeling bad that she couldn't invite him in.

"Sure."

With a final smile, Bronte shut the door. An evening with Ryan would have been fun, she thought, but swiftly reminded herself that her dream man would be arriving very soon and their 'laid-back' date wasn't going to arrange itself!

She finished getting ready and then went into the kitchen and began preparing the risotto. She put some jazz music on low, keeping one ear listening out for Sebastian, and poured herself a glass of wine.

She could hear Mr Darcy already getting restless in the room above and decided to take him up his dinner. She used her elbow to pull down the handle and open the bedroom door, her hands full with the cat's water bowl and food. Of course, Sebastian had to choose that exact moment to knock.

"Come in, it's open!" called out Bronte over her shoulder.

With a petulant yowl, Mr Darcy shot past her and down the stairs.

Spotting his nemesis, Mr Darcy stopped in his tracks and growled menacingly. Sebastian looked petrified and took a slow cautious step backwards, back over the threshold.

"Mr Darcy!" said Bronte as commandingly as she could. She received a hiss in return. The cat didn't take his eyes off Sebastian. His ears lay flat against his head.

Bronte shook the food bowl she still had in her hand and his ears pricked.

"Come on, sweetheart," she said soothingly, rattling the food again.

This time the cat turned his head.

"That's the way," continued Bronte, "yummy food for my hungry boy . . ."

Mr Darcy gave Sebastian a final glare, and swishing his tail indignantly, sauntered back up the stairs. Bronte lowered the bowl and shook it again, anxious to keep his attention on it.

Daring to take her eyes off the cat for a moment, Bronte glanced at Sebastian. He still hadn't moved.

As the animal got closer Bronte inched back into the bedroom, keeping the food low to lure Mr Darcy in. When she'd made it into the middle of the room, she put the water and food bowls on the floor. She had no idea how she was going to get past Mr Darcy and close the door without him getting out and threatening poor Sebastian again, but luckily Mr Darcy's natural greediness took over and he began tucking into his dinner like he didn't have a care in the world.

Knowing that she'd be pushing her luck if she so much as caught the cat's eye, Bronte scurried out of the room and shut the door firmly behind her.

Bronte took a deep breath and went down the stairs. Sebastian was still standing outside on the front step.

"You can come in now," she said, just about managing to suppress her smile.

"What have you done with it?" asked Sebastian, peering apprehensively inside the house.

"He's closed in one of the bedrooms." Seeing the panic flooding Sebastian's face, she quickly added, "Don't worry, he can't get out."

"Oh, OK," said Sebastian, with one final glance up the stairs he pulled himself together now he knew his legs and trousers were no longer in immediate danger.

"Let's go through to the kitchen and I'll get you a drink, supper must be almost ready. Oh blast, I hope nothing's burnt! I really am sorry about my cat, he can be a grumpy old thing, but I've never known him to take such a dislike to someone. Maybe he's jealous!" she laughed, trying to lighten the atmosphere as she hurried over to the stove.

"Maybe," Sebastian agreed weakly.

Bronte managed to rescue the risotto by swiftly adding some more stock and giving it a good stir.

Sebastian sat down at the table but still looked a bit twitchy. Bronte thought it best to get a glass of wine in his hands.

"Red or white," she asked, holding two bottles up.

"Err, red, please."

Bronte poured him a large glass of Argentinean Malbec. He downed half of it immediately. The alcohol seemed to restore a little of the lost colour to his cheeks, but an awkward hush fell over the kitchen.

Serving the food, Bronte brought their meals over and joined Sebastian at the table.

"I hope you like risotto," she said.

"Lovely, thanks," replied Sebastian, looking at his plate suspiciously and pushing the rice around with his fork.

They ate in silence until Bronte felt forced to ask the inevitable, "So, how's polo training going?"

The sluice gate opened and Sebastian was soon in full flow, filling her in about every second of his last practice session. He was describing what had happened when he'd brought his new pony out for the first time when he stopped abruptly, "What was that?" he said urgently.

"Sorry?" asked Bronte, coming out of her polo-induced trance.

"That noise. Sounds like scratching. Listen!"

Bronte listened for a moment and was just about to suggest Sebastian had been imagining things when she too heard scratching, followed by a small thump.

"It'll just be Mr Darcy. He probably doesn't think much of being cooped up. Or maybe he can smell you and is still hungry," she teased, but regretted her words as soon as she'd said them: Sebastian looked stricken.

"I'm only joking!" she said, "You're quite safe, he can't get out."

Sebastian didn't appear to be paying her any attention and was shovelling in the last few mouthfuls of risotto.

The final forkful was washed down with the last of the wine and Sebastian pushed back his chair and said, "I'm ever so sorry, Bronte, but I'm afraid I'm going to have to go."

"Oh! Um, OK. What a pity."

"Yes . . . not feeling too well. I'm sure it's nothing serious, but . . . um . . ."

"Is there anything I can do?" Bronte asked.

"No, I'm afraid not. Think I'd better just get home," he replied, already making his way into the hall and putting his coat on.

Bronte opened the front door and he went out but stopped on the step. "I'll call you and we'll arrange something else soon," he said, lifting her chin up gently. She melted as his gaze met hers and his lips moved towards her. Desire filled Bronte as she anticipated a kiss to rival that at the end of their last date. Suddenly there was another bang and a yowl from upstairs. Sebastian jumped back in alarm and mumbled, "I'll be in touch," as he raced back to his car.

Bronte watched him drive off. She sighed, what a disaster! Surely the start of a relationship, if that's even what it was, shouldn't be this difficult! This ought to be the fun bit! Bloody Mr Darcy! Why couldn't he have behaved?

Bronte stomped up the stairs. She'd better let the silly creature out if she didn't want him destroying her guest room. She went in cautiously, not quite sure what to expect, but the cat was sitting calmly on the bed, placidly looking out of the window.

Bronte gave him her sternest look, "Mr Darcy! You really aren't helping things! Sebastian hasn't done anything to you, and I was looking forward to this evening."

Her little speech was rewarded with a hiss, but she continued with a firm, "Sebastian's going to be around here a lot, so you'd better just get used to him!"

He looked completely unabashed, so Bronte decided to give up her reprimand. It was still early, she'd get some work done, although she didn't think she'd add Sebastian's fear of her cat to her hero's traits!

* * *

Bronte struggled along with her manuscript; it really wasn't coming as easily as she'd thought it would. She was doing her best to write a romance, but leaving out any real interaction between the two protagonists as they just didn't seem to gel. Whatever she tried, Angus and Pippa did not get along! They seemed to annoy each other a lot of the time and had wildly differing opinions on absolutely everything.

On the evening of her next writing-group meeting her ankle was feeling a lot better; she was able to drive and was looking forward to getting out of the house. She hoped talking through the problem with her friends might help her find a way through it.

She printed off what she had of her new book and was all ready to go, but when she went to start her Mini, it was having none of it. She got back out of the car again and noticed a smell of petrol hanging in the air. "Great," she thought, "What am I going to do now?" She knocked on Ryan's front door; she'd heard him come home from work a little earlier so knew he was in.

"Hi, Bronte, you OK?" he said when he saw her.

"My car won't start. It was fine yesterday, but now it's completely dead and I can smell petrol. Do you have a minute to take a look? I'm hoping it's something really simple and I'm just being a bit useless!"

"Sure. Let me grab my coat and a torch."

Ryan poked and prodded about for a bit while Bronte held the light for him. After a couple of minutes he extracted himself from under the bonnet, cleaned his hands on a cloth, and gave his verdict: "It looks like the fuel line's leaked pretty badly, see the puddle of petrol over there? I can patch it up for you so you can take it to a garage, but not until tomorrow morning, it would be impossible to do in the dark."

"Ryan, you're amazing — thanks so much. Won't it be a lot of work? Are you sure you don't mind?"

"No, it's no trouble. My uncle's a mechanic and he taught me a fair bit about engines. Honestly, it won't take long tomorrow. But it'll still have to go into the garage soon — what I can do isn't going to last. The whole fuel line will need replacing by the look of things."

Bronte took her bag out of the car and locked the door.

"Where were you heading? Do you need a lift?"

"I was supposed to be meeting Camille and some other writers for our meet up in the Swan. I was hoping they might be able to solve a problem I'm having with my new book."

"Would you like me to drive you?"

"Oh no! I can't take up more of your evening than I already have!"

"You wouldn't be. I'll even bring you back home: the cupboard's bare, I'll take a book and their pie and mash is legendary."

"OK, but I'll be finished by about nine, we can eat together then if you want? I'll treat you to the pie and mash as a thank you."

"Sounds like a plan to me," said Ryan with a huge grin. His smile was infectious, and Bronte immediately found herself returning it, light-hearted once more.

* * *

"A different man every meeting, eh?" Bernard said cheekily as Bronte and Ryan approached the group.

"Ryan's my neighbour. My car's not working so he kindly drove me here," said Bronte, keen to ensure no one got the wrong idea about her and Ryan.

"A likely story!" muttered Bernard.

"What would you like to drink?" Bronte asked Ryan.

"Just an orange juice, thanks. I never drink when I'm driving. I'll be over there," he said, pointing to the far corner of the room.

"Don't be daft, son!" said Bernard, "You can't sit all the way over there by yourself. Come and join us."

Ryan turned to Bronte, his eyes asking if it was alright for him to hang around. She gave a little 'sure' shrug.

"I wouldn't want to intrude or be in the way."

"You won't be! I'm working on my gardening memoirs, and I've brought along the chapter about how I won first prize for my marrow at the county fair back in '86. I'd love your opinion on it," Bernard assured him, taking Ryan's arm proprietorially and launching into a tale of skulduggery and compost.

For a moment, Ryan looked like he might be regretting bringing Bronte, but he good-naturedly sat down next to Bernard and was being introduced to the other members of the group as Bronte slipped away to get their drinks.

Bronte thought having Ryan at the meeting might make things a little awkward, but no one seemed unduly bothered by his being there. In fact, Bernard appeared to have recruited Ryan as his new best friend. Bronte heard him offering to email Ryan some of his poetry that he thought Ryan might particularly enjoy.

As it neared Bronte's turn to read her work, she found herself tapping her feet nervously. She wasn't sure she wanted Ryan to hear her rough first draft. Her little group were all fellow authors, all in the same boat, but Ryan was an outsider. What if he hated her writing?

So what? answered a voice in her head. What difference does it make what he thinks of your work? Bronte knew the sort of novels she wrote were never going to win big literary awards, but she was good at what she did, and was proud of her books — people enjoyed them: they were accessible to everyone, light and warm, they weren't pretentious or stuffy, but were fun, full of life, humour and, more than anything, love — love, the oldest and best story of them all. But despite telling herself this, she respected Ryan's opinion, and hated the thought that he might mentally file her books away under 'Sentimental Nonsense' and consider them beneath him.

And what if he realised her hero, Angus, was based on Sebastian — which hardly required the deductive powers of Poirot?

That could be embarrassing!

When she began reading, she was very careful not to make eye contact with Ryan. She focussed on the paper in front of her. She finished and muttered an apologetic, "That's where I get a bit stuck."

"Writer's block," declared Bernard sagely. "Don't hold with it myself, but there are plenty who do."

"I can write, just not scenes when my hero and heroine are together. They don't really get along very well!"

"The classic love-hate relationship! You'll sort them out!" said Camille.

"It's not so much love-hate as that they don't seem to have very much in common and my heroine isn't terribly interested in my hero. I know that sounds a bit silly," she continued, addressing Ryan now more than her colleagues, "They're fictitious, purely a figment of my imagination, but when I write, my characters become almost real, and carry the story away, take it where it needs to go. Or else, well, it doesn't matter how good the plot is, the tale just doesn't tell itself."

Several heads nodded in agreement, and suggestions were made:

"Perhaps they just need to be thrown together a bit more? Given the chance to overcome their differences?"

"Could he take an interest in something she cares about?"

"Maybe your hero isn't right for your heroine," Ryan commented quietly.

"But he's perfect!" Bronte said without pausing for thought.

"Maybe he's not perfect for her," Ryan replied.

The conversation moved on, but Bronte went over and over Ryan's observation in her mind. Was he right? Surely her new hero was the archetype of what every woman wanted: confident, commanding, handsome and extremely wealthy. It's what sold books, and what her readers went to bed dreaming about. Why wouldn't her heroine want him?

* * *

The meeting ended with the group succeeding in getting Ryan to pledge that he'd come to the next — both to Bronte's delight and chagrin. Ryan and Bronte retired to a smaller table and ordered the promised beef-and-ale pies and mash.

"I was a bit nervous about reading my work out in front of you," Bronte admitted.

"Why?"

"Well, it was quite rough, and you're not really my target audience. I wasn't sure what you'd think of it."

"I've read some of your stuff."

"You have?"

"Yep. The Laird's Heir and Her Highland Master."

Bronte wasn't sure what to say. Ryan left her hanging for a minute, then added with a smile, "I thought they were brilliant."

"Seriously?"

"Yes. I admit they're not my usual sort of read, but your writing style was great. I loved all the twists and turns, the little intrigues."

"Why didn't you tell me you'd read them, before?"

"I don't know. Maybe I was worried you'd think it a bit weird that I was reading them. But I was just interested in what you do. You're very talented."

"Thank you! That means a lot."

"How did you get into writing?"

"Are you sure you really want to hear about this?" asked Bronte, thinking especially of Sebastian's singular lack of interest in anything to do with her or her work.

"Of course, I wouldn't ask otherwise."

"Well, after university I went to work for a romance publisher. My job was to sift through all the many, many manuscripts sent in and pick out the ones that showed promise. To be honest, at times it could be pretty dispiriting — some of what we received was seriously bad, but then, every now and again, there'd be a plot that really stood out as something special. After reading through literally hundreds of submissions, I knew what made a great story and I figured I must have a pretty good idea of what would sell and how to write it. I wrote like crazy during the evenings and weekends until I had a finished romance novel. I showed it to one of the editors and, almost before I knew it, I had a contract. I wrote my first four books while still working full-time, but then I gave up my job, left London and moved out here."

"That was quite a leap of faith — I'm definitely more of a 'know exactly what's coming into the bank at the end of the month' kind of person!"

"I was too, but . . . well . . . I'd just broken up with my long-term boyfriend and, I guess, I really needed a change."

"Do you think you made the right decision?"

"Absolutely," she replied without hesitation. "I love writing, I love my home, and, as you saw tonight, I've made some brilliant friends here."

"They seem like a great bunch."

"They are. They're so supportive. I might have gone a little crazy working by myself if it weren't for them."

Bronte took a sip of her drink, and asked, a little more out of politeness than real interest, "How did you get into dentistry?"

Ryan guffawed, "You know, not many people ask that. They tend to ask why on earth I wanted to go into dentistry!"

Bronte smiled. "Well, maybe that as well. I mean, there can't be that many kids who long to become a dentist."

"No, I suppose not."

"But then what do kids know, eh?"

"Exactly! The youth of today have no idea just how sexy teeth and gums are."

"Fools! All that flossing. The glory of root canals. I don't know what they're thinking of, daydreaming about becoming footballers and pop stars."

They both laughed.

"My dad's a dentist," Ryan said. "I guess I always just looked up to him. He's the only dentist in the town I grew up in and I liked seeing how he helped people. He's so good, I think it's the only place in the world where no one is afraid of going to the dentist."

"How come you didn't join his practice and work with him?"

"As much as I love him, I think that working with my dad every day would quickly lose its appeal. Especially as I'd most likely be stuck mixing up fillings as everyone would insist on seeing the 'senior dentist.' I wanted to strike out on my own."

They both ordered coffees and deliciously rich sticky-toffee puddings, and continued chatting easily until they heard the barman calling last orders. Bronte couldn't believe it was that late and checked her watch.

"We'd better get going before we're kicked out," said Ryan.

Walking to the car, Bronte liked how Ryan fussed over her, offering her his arm to hold, checking her ankle wasn't hurting, and opening the car door for her. It felt rather old-fashioned, but nice. She did worry that Ryan might still be hoping for more than friendship — he did perhaps treat her as a caring boyfriend might. But what could she do? She'd been completely honest with him about how she felt, and about Sebastian. She truly valued their friendship, and it was great having someone so warm and helpful in the cottage next door. Maybe she ought to talk about Sebastian more, to make it completely clear she was off the market, so to speak. The problem was that he seemed to vanish from her mind when she and Ryan were chatting away. But that was probably because things were still so new between her and Sebastian. They were sensible to be taking things slowly, and she knew she'd be a fool not to give everything to make them work as a couple. Sebastian was exactly what she'd spent so long looking for.

Determined to remind Ryan that they really were just friends, she allowed him to help her up the garden path and admonish her gently for not using the walking stick he'd given her, but shook his hand as they parted, ensuring there could be no misinterpreted goodbye hug or peck on the cheek.

Ryan gave her a small, almost sad, smile. She was sure he knew what her actions meant, which was exactly what she wanted. But it didn't feel very nice, or very natural, to leave him like that.

CHAPTER SIX

Camille popped by for a cup of tea the next morning. Ryan had left for work, having done the temporary fix on Bronte's car. She was clearly curious to hear how things had panned out in the pub after she'd left.

"It was great having Ryan at the meeting last night, wasn't it? I would not have thought inviting an outsider would work, but it seemed to. Did you guys have a nice time afterwards?" Camille asked with a grin.

"We ate pie and mash and chatted. It was fun."

"Pie and mash? That's not very romantic."

"It wasn't a date. As I've explained, Ryan was just doing me a favour bringing me."

"So, are you absolutely sure you're not interested in him?"

"Absolutely, positively."

"Any particular reason why?"

"Aside from the fact that I'm dating Sebastian?"

"Yes."

"And the dentist thing?"

"I thought you'd be over that by now . . ."

"He's a bit short."

"So is Tom Cruise."

"The hair?"

"Is cute!"

"OK, maybe the height and the hair are fine, but I'm not backing down about the job. And don't you think he's a bit, well, sensible?"

"And what's so terrible about that?"

"Sensible's boring, isn't it? No one wants to spend their life with sensible," said Bronte without conviction.

"Do you find Ryan boring? I certainly don't, and I'm sure there are plenty of other women who agree with me."

"Let them go out with him, then!"

"If you're not careful, one of them will, and I suspect you'll be rather sorry."

"I won't be. Ryan's fantastic, he's a great friend, but he just doesn't compare to Sebastian romantically."

"I'll concede that Sebastian is very suave and handsome, but things aren't exactly serious between the two of you yet, are they? I wouldn't rule Ryan out completely if I were you."

"You know I'm a one-man kind of girl, Camille, and Sebastian's the man for me. I know it. I'm happy to take things slowly, there's no rush, we're just getting to know each other."

"Cherie, so long as you're happy, I'm happy. But only if I get to be maid of honour when you marry Sebastian in some enormous society wedding covered by *Hello* magazine, OK?"

"I'm sure that can be arranged," Bronte laughed, glad to have moved away from the topic of Ryan.

* * *

Bronte's writing went better over the next couple of days. Her conversation with Camille had given her an idea: she decided to introduce a new character who would make her hero Angus appear even more attractive: a younger and far less glamorous and exciting brother: Douglas. She was tempted to give him some really mundane, dreary occupation. A dentist equivalent. But didn't want to offend Ryan if he read it.

Douglas would come to the castle and basically showcase how great the hero was. Maybe he could even have an evil streak. She wrote the brother's arrival and planned to have him working a lot and generally being rather dull. The castle could be in danger of being sold, and Douglas would be all in favour of it. Her hero and heroine would work together to save the family home and discover their love for each other!

The storyline was really beginning to come together, and she was loving writing her new character.

* * *

Bronte was packing up her laptop late Friday afternoon and considering popping next door to see if Ryan fancied a film and a curry, when a text came through on her mobile. Her heart beat a little faster when she saw it was from Sebastian.

Dinner at my house tomorrow at seven? it read.

Bronte grinned to herself: they'd emailed back and forth since their last, rather disastrous date, but hadn't met up since. She'd been getting a bit worried that Sebastian might be losing interest.

Lovely, can I bring anything? she replied.

Only yourself.

See you then! she texted back immediately. A romantic meal for two (and no grumpy cat) was just what they needed to get them back on track. She wondered if he would cook. Probably not, she decided, he'd have someone to do that for him.

She was straight on the phone to Camille. "What should I wear?" she asked her fashion-minded friend.

"You're spending the evening in a genuine stately home, you'd better dress up. They all change for dinner."

"Are you sure you haven't been watching too much Downton Abbey?"

"Well you're not going to turn up in jogging trousers and a sweatshirt, are you? The butler will think you're there to clean out the horses and got lost on the way to the stables!"

"That's a fair point . . ."

"Why don't I bring some outfits by tomorrow for you to try on?"

"You're at least a dress size smaller than me, I'll never fit into them!"

"Don't worry, I can find a few things to suit you! I can be with you at about four."

"Thanks Camille, that would be brilliant. It's really kind of you; I so want tomorrow night to go well."

"It will. This time next year you'll be laughing about this as you twiddle your huge diamond engagement ring."

"Stop making me more nervous!"

"Sorry!" Camille laughed, "I'll see you tomorrow."

"OK! Thanks again."

Bronte abandoned the idea of going to see Ryan — she was so excited, she doubted she'd be able to concentrate on a film, and a takeaway was definitely a bad idea if she hoped to have any chance of fitting into one of Camille's tiny dresses the following evening. She tidied up, made some supper, then read until bedtime, all the while resisting the urge to scrawl Bronte Huntington-Fairfax all over her writing pad.

* * *

As promised, Camille arrived at four the next afternoon. She meant business: it took several trips back and forth to her car to unload the huge selection of dresses and bags of make-up she'd brought with her.

"Come on, then," she hustled Bronte up the stairs to her bedroom. "Let's get some of these tried on."

Finally, an hour and a half later, Camille thought they'd found Bronte the perfect outfit. The black beaded cocktail dress was gorgeous. It was classy, yet showed exactly the right amount of leg. But there was one slight problem: it was rather tight.

"How will I sit down in this?" Bronte bemoaned.

"Just stand as much as you can," Camille suggested. Her French ancestry meant she had a rather 'smile through the pain' approach to fashion: no heel was too high for her.

"But I'm going to dinner! I'm going to have to sit down!"

Camille grinned. "Get dinner over and done with as quickly as you can, then move on to something that could involve the dress being taken off."

"What if I burst a seam?"

"You won't burst a seam! This is Parisian couture. Parisian couture seams do not burst."

"Alright, alright, I believe you." Bronte turned once again in front of the mirror. "Don't you think I'll be cold?" she added, noticing the goosebumps already appearing on her arms.

"The place will be full of roaring fires."

The look on Bronte's face suggested she wasn't completely convinced, so Camille threw her a cashmere wrap. "Put this over the top if you're worried. Right, let's get on with your make-up!"

"Thanks so much for this."

"It's not a problem at all. I never get to dress up properly anymore, stuck out here: I'm living vicariously. Anyway, what are friends for?"

* * *

Camille left at twenty to seven, wishing Bronte luck and extracting a promise that she'd call the next morning to tell her everything.

Bronte gave herself a final once-over before grabbing her bag and car keys and setting off for the Fenworth Estate. Camille had suggested Bronte take a cab so she could enjoy a couple of glasses of wine, but for some reason Bronte felt she wanted the car with her. She was pretty independent and liked to know she could leave whenever she wanted to. Not that she anticipated wanting to bail out early of course, but she wanted the option.

She climbed rather gingerly into her old Mini, acutely aware of just how tight her dress was.

It was a cold evening and her car, which she hadn't used for a couple of days was reluctant to start. Hearing she was having trouble, Ryan came out of his house to see if she needed any help. When he saw her outfit he muttered a quiet "Wow," then added, "You look fantastic."

"Thanks. I'm supposed to be going out for dinner with Sebastian at Fenworth, but it'll all be for nothing if I can't get this stupid thing started."

Ryan frowned slightly, but seemed to shake it off. "Let me take a look," he said, opening the bonnet. "Did you take it to the garage?"

"Um, no, sorry, I haven't had a chance. I got a bit caught up in work."

Ryan muttered darkly to himself as he worked silently for a moment and then called out, "Try it now."

Bronte turned the key in the ignition and the engine miraculously burst into life.

"Oh, thank you!" Bronte cheered.

"Are you sure you want to take it out? You might find it dead again when you go to restart it. It really needs to be checked over properly by a mechanic."

"I'll risk it, I'm already running late. I promise I'll take it to the garage on Monday."

"OK, but drive carefully."

"I will. Thanks again!" she called out, anxious to be off.

* * *

The car seemed to be running fairly well, and Bronte drove it as hard as she thought it could take, but by the time she pulled up outside Fenworth she was ten minutes late. She took a moment to compose herself, not wanting to knock on the door all hot and bothered.

She'd actually been to the house once before: she and Camille had come here the previous year for a small Christmas Fair. The estate had been selling freshly cut Christmas trees and she'd bought a beautiful, enormously bushy six-foot one. Then she'd practically had to beg the extremely grumpy man selling them to give her a hand getting it onto the roof of her

Mini. It's not like he'd had any other customers waiting — the paddock had been deserted and no one could exactly run off with one!

And she'd discovered later that he'd overcharged her.

The house itself had been full of life for the fair: lights on everywhere, people milling around, the festive stalls spilling out onto the forecourt, and the great front doors open invitingly. The air had been heavy with the scent of pine needles and mulled wine.

Now the house looked forlorn and abandoned. So much so, that the thought went through Bronte's mind that she might have got the wrong night and Sebastian wasn't here. But surely the butler, the cook, and whoever else there was to help run the huge house would be around? Unless they'd been given the evening off. Or maybe they were all in the staff quarters?

She chuckled to herself as she realised her ideas were taken straight from all the television dramas and films she'd watched set in stately homes, most of them Jane Austen adaptations!

It was so dark that she struggled to make her way up the stone steps to the large, extremely imposing entrance. She finally located the knocker and banged it. The noise seemed to reverberate through the whole house. She waited. Nothing. She was hunting in her bag for her mobile to call Sebastian and find out where he was, when a light came on and shone through the narrow windows on either side of the arched gothic frame.

Finally, Sebastian opened the doors.

"Darling, you're here!" he proclaimed and kissed Bronte.

"Sorry, I'm a bit late. Car trouble," she explained.

"Not to worry, come on through. May I take your coat? You look nice!"

Bronte handed the garment over, but immediately regretted doing so: the house was absolutely freezing. Something else dawned on her: she was extremely overdressed compared to Sebastian — goodness, how many layers was he wearing?

He must have had at least two thick jumpers on and was even wearing a scarf!

It also clicked that Sebastian had opened the door himself: didn't this sort of place usually have a butler or a doorman or someone to do that? Perhaps he'd been worried she might feel intimidated by their stuffy old butler so had made sure he let her in personally.

Pulling her wrap close around her, she followed him through into the main hall. A huge, dramatically sweeping staircase faced them, but they walked around it and Sebastian led her down some rather dimly lit corridors. The house didn't look nearly as impressive as it had for the Christmas Fair — then there'd been distinguished-looking portraits, glittering chandeliers, thick curtains in deep golds and greens, and a cheerful blaze burning in the fireplace of every room. The windows had sparkled in the weak winter sunlight. There hadn't been much in the way of rugs or furniture, but Bronte had just assumed they'd been moved to make room for the stalls or so they didn't get accidentally damaged by all the visitors.

The rooms they passed now all seemed unused. The fire grates were empty. The walls and windows were bare. The little furniture there was, lay covered in dust sheets.

"Don't you use all the rooms downstairs?" Bronte asked.

"Good lord, no, terribly draughty. We usually only open them up when we're holding an event. To be honest, we don't spend much time here outside the shooting season. It's rather dull to be stuck out in the sticks."

"Oh," said Bronte surprised. Shooting? He couldn't mean shooting actual animals, could he? He wouldn't do that! They must use those clay pigeon things, she told herself hopefully.

Finally, they went through a doorway and down a narrow, musty staircase to reach the kitchen.

The room was large and seemed, if possible, even colder than the rest of the building. An odd smell permeated the air, bringing to mind rain-soaked, sweaty Wellington boots drying on a hot radiator.

Sat at a long pine table was a sour-faced man. An equally miserable-looking woman stood stirring a large pan at the stove. They turned to stare at Bronte and Sebastian as they came into the room. They were dressed almost identically in moth-eaten woollen jumpers and thick corduroy trousers, very similar in fact to Sebastian's. Bronte recognised the man as the rude chap who'd swindled her over the Christmas tree. Perhaps they were the cook and butler? They weren't very smartly turned out, but then it was so cold that Sebastian probably let them dress like that to keep warm.

"Bronte, meet Mummy and Daddy. Mummy and Daddy — Bronte."

Bronte hoped she managed to cover her surprise quickly enough as she stepped forward to greet Sebastian's parents. She held out her hand briefly to his father, but all she received in return was a sort of grunt before he carried on reading the newspaper, all but disappearing behind it. She moved towards Sebastian's mother, who shook her hand, barely taking her eyes off the stove.

"It's a pleasure to meet you . . ." Bronte said.

"You may call us Lord and Lady Fairfax," Sebastian's mother said stiffly.

"Right . . ." replied Bronte, not quite sure what to say or do with herself. She was saved by Sebastian, his head inside a large drinks cabinet, calling out, "Anyone for a snifter?"

"Yes, thank you, dear," replied his mother.

"Large!" came a growl from behind the newspaper.

"Sorry?" asked Bronte.

"A snifter? You know, a little pre-dinner tipple. Mummy and Daddy'll have a gin and tonic, but mine's a vodka."

"Oh! Could I have a small vodka and tonic, please? I'm driving," she explained. The glass, when presented, was what she would have termed 'very large indeed', but in all fairness to Sebastian, it was only about a third of the size of what he'd prepared for his mother and father. She gamely took a sip and gave an involuntary shudder: it tasted like neat vodka.

"Is your drink alright?" asked Sebastian.

"Er . . . Yes, thank you. It's just a little stronger than I'm used to."

A derisive snort came from the newspaper.

Fed up with standing around, but not sure what to do with herself and feeling ridiculous in her cocktail dress and heels, Bronte decided to take matters into her own hands. She'd now deduced that no one was going to offer her a seat. She sat down anyway, before her tired ankle gave out on her. The chair she chose, being the furthest from Lord Fairfax, screeched horribly on the flagstones as she pulled it out from under the table, and all eyes turned to look at her.

"Sorry," she mumbled.

The conversation, which they'd presumably been having before she arrived, recommenced around her as if she weren't there. Sebastian and his father discussed some tenants who were struggling to pay their rent. Lady Fairfax chimed in every so often. "Just tell them to leave! Take the dogs with you so they know you mean business," she advised her husband.

Appalled, Bronte focussed on her horrid drink, taking tiny sips and trying to think of a way to dispose of the rest without causing offence.

Eventually, Lady Fairfax announced, "Supper's almost ready. Could you sort out some more drinks, Sebastian dear? I think there's a bottle of the '98 claret in the pantry."

"Wine for you, Bronte?"

"I can't, I'm driving."

Why had she accepted that awful vodka and tonic she thought, she would have much rather had a little glass of the wine.

"Can I do anything to help?" she asked.

"You can cut the bread," answered Lady Fairfax, indicating a small loaf on a board next to her. "The bread knife's in the drawer by the kettle."

Bronte set to work on the loaf, but it was hard as rock and the knife was blunt. She finally resorted to a mixture of a frantic hacking motion with the knife and tearing the loaf apart with her hands. By the time she'd finished her task the rest of the meal had been served.

Bronte brought the mangled slices over to the table and sat back down. She was pretty hungry by now, but her appetite rapidly disappeared once she saw what was on her plate and the source of the peculiar welly aroma was revealed.

"You're in for a treat tonight!" said Sebastian cheerfully, "There's nothing quite like one of Mummy's home-cooked suppers."

You're right about that, thought Bronte. The meal was some sort of meat stew. It was grey and a firm layer of grease was congealing rapidly on the surface as it cooled. Next to it was a pile of mashed potato, the lumps so prominent they could be seen sticking out of the sides. Peas were also served. At least Bronte assumed they had once been peas, but they'd been cooked for so long they were a sort of sludgy mush.

"This looks delicious, thank you," she said politely. She tried to remember all the tricks she used to call into play as a child to make it look like she'd eaten more of her vegetables than she actually had.

She surreptitiously looked around to check what everyone else was doing with their food, hoping she had an ally, but the three of them were tucking in like they hadn't eaten for a week.

Oh well, at least it's warm, she consoled herself as she took a big forkful, closed her eyes and put it in her mouth; here goes nothing! It was just unfortunate that Lord Fairfax chose that precise moment to hold up a piece of his stew and ask, "Is this heart or kidney do you think?"

* * *

The rest of the dinner passed very slowly. Bronte found she could just about stomach the stew if she mixed a small amount of it with a much larger amount of the mash and peas and then took a gulp of water to wash it down. She managed half of it before she could convincingly admit defeat and dishonestly declared herself, "Full to bursting."

Bronte's hopes that she could fill up on dessert were dashed when the table was cleared and Sebastian asked if she'd like to move into the drawing room with him. Clutching the mug of instant coffee he'd made her when she'd turned down another vodka and tonic, she luxuriated in the feeling of her fingers defrosting as they took in the heat.

This new room was also large and draughty, and in her rather skimpy outfit, Bronte was actually beginning to shiver. She sat down as carefully as she could on a chaise longue, painfully aware of her dress, which was so tight it seemed to be squeezing her ribs. She'd never have believed she'd be thinking it, but she was desperate for the evening to end. How soon until she could politely make her excuses?

"I didn't realise we'd be eating with your parents," she said, making an effort to initiate conversation.

"If you want a decent meal around here, it comes from Mummy!"

"So does your mother do all the cooking?"

"Yah. We had Cookie when I was little, but we got rid of her when she made a lasagne. Daddy doesn't like foreign food."

"What about the rest of the housework? Surely your mother doesn't do all that herself as well. This place is huge!"

"Oh no, a girl comes in to clean. But we generally use very few rooms here. We spend most of the year at the Mayfair house. We've been trying to sell this place for ages."

"Oh no! Isn't there something that could be done to save it?" said Bronte, immediately thinking of the plot of her book, and envisaging Sebastian desperately doing everything he could to rescue his beloved ancestral home and protect the tenants from eviction. The image rapidly dissolved when he answered, "We're thinking about building on some of the land and turning the rest of the old place into a hotel and golf course, but getting planning permission is terribly tricky."

"Oh."

"There's a developer coming to look around next week, so we'll see what he says."

Bronte struggled to raise an encouraging smile. Life at Fenworth was turning out to be very different from what she'd expected, and she was finding it hard to hide her disappointment.

"So, how's the polo going?" she asked, anxious to change the subject.

"Good, the team's working well. We had a long training session today in fact. I tried out a pony I'm considering buying and . . ."

"But what will happen to your horses if you sell this house?"

"We have stables in London we use. Most of the horses are kept there now anyway. It's actually closer to where we train. You know, only last week . . ."

He droned on . . . and on . . . and on. Bronte tried to be courteous and pay attention, but by now she was so cold she worried her teeth would start chattering. She was hungry, yet still feeling slightly queasy from dinner, and her dress was too constricting. The fact that the company was also dire tipped her over the edge. Taking advantage of a brief hiatus in his monologue as he turned his attention to his vodka and tonic, she interjected, "Thank you for a lovely evening. I'm afraid I ought to go now."

"Oh, what a shame! Are you sure you can't stay longer? You're welcome to spend the night," he said with an inviting smile.

"I'm sorry. My cat needs feeding and I don't like driving late at night, I really should go."

"Alright, well at least let me walk you to your car."

They made their way back through the house in silence. In her desperation for some form of warmth, Bronte almost snatched her coat from Sebastian when he handed it to her. She put it on, but it didn't make much difference, as it had been hanging in the freezing hallway for the last couple of hours. It was practically stiff with the cold. Didn't they heat this part of the house at all?

Outside actually seemed a couple of degrees warmer, and she didn't think she'd ever been so happy to see her little car. She could hardly wait to get inside it and put her heater on. In twenty minutes she would be home and in her pyjamas, with a cup of tea and a plate of buttery toast.

She was reaching down to put her key in the lock when Sebastian turned her to face him. However anxious she was to get home, she still couldn't help going a little weak at the knees as his dreamy eyes met hers. He leant in and kissed her on her lips, then stroked her cheek gently with his fingers.

"I hope to see you again soon. Mummy and Daddy loved meeting you. Mummy adores anyone who appreciates her cooking."

"Great, it was really interesting to meet them," said Bronte, trying to keep her answer as honest as possible, but without causing offence.

She got into her car and went to start the engine. It spluttered slightly for a few seconds and then cut out completely. Oh no, please not now, Bronte silently prayed.

Sebastian tapped on the window and she wound it down.

"Your car playing up?"

"Looks like it."

"I can drive you home if you like, or you could reconsider staying here? We've got plenty of room."

"You can't drive me, you've had too much to drink."

"Well, I guess you're staying, then. Come on, I'll make us a hot toddy to warm you up. It's chilly out here."

Despair washed over Bronte. What was she going to do? She'd never survive a whole night in that freezing house! They'd find her turned into an icicle in the morning. If she did make it through, she could just imagine the joy on Lady Fairfax's face when she saw Bronte sat at the breakfast table the next morning.

She contemplated calling a cab, but she was pretty much in the middle of nowhere so it would take a while to get to her and would be expensive. She didn't have much cash on her or back at the cottage and it was a bit cheeky to ask for a loan from Sebastian.

Resigning herself to a hypothermia-inducing night at Fenworth, she could have laughed with joy when her phone rang and she saw it was Ryan calling her.

"Just a second," she said to Sebastian, "I need to take this, it's my neighbour."

"Ryan!" she answered.

"Hiya, sorry to interrupt your evening. I just wanted to check it was alright for me to take Mr Darcy into my house for the night, he won't stop yowling outside my window."

"I'm so sorry! The silly cat flap must have stuck, of course you can bring him in, or give the cat flap a shove to open it for him. Actually, I was about to leave and I would have been home soon, but the engine's died again."

"I'll sort out Mr Darcy's private entrance for him. Would you like me to come and get you? I doubt I'll be able to get your car started tonight, but I can drive you home and you could get it towed to a garage tomorrow — I'm afraid I don't have a tow rope, else I'd bring it back for you tonight."

There was a part of Bronte that knew she ought to turn down his very kind offer: it was late and cold, he shouldn't have to come out and pick her up. Plus she really should have taken her car to the garage before, as he'd advised her to. But she longed to be back in her cosy little cottage. Another look at her alternative home for the night — dark, gloomy and foreboding, its outline vaguely silhouetted in the faint moonlight — made up her mind.

"If you're sure you don't mind, that would be brilliant. Do you know where Fenworth is?"

"I'll type it into the satnav. I'll be with you soon, keep warm."

"I will. Thanks."

Sebastian must have overheard most of the conversation and didn't look best pleased with the turn of events.

"Would you like to come back inside to wait?" he asked somewhat sullenly.

Bronte would have rather stayed in the car, but wasn't going to make things more awkward than they already were. She followed him back into the house, along the hallways returning to the kitchen, making stilted conversation about her car problems. Bronte was grateful the room was empty, Sebastian's mother and father had presumably gone to bed.

"May I make you another coffee?" Sebastian asked.

"No, I'm fine thanks," she answered, praying she wouldn't be there long enough to drink it.

Gosh, this is difficult, Bronte thought as the uncomfortable atmosphere resumed, not at all as I'd imagined an evening with Sebastian would be.

"Oh, I forgot to say: we're having a bit of a ball here in a couple of weeks. Midwinter sort of thing. Do it every year. I was hoping you'd come, as my date."

"Wow, that sounds amazing," she perked up, "of course I'll come."

"I'll be in London from Monday, but I'll text you the details. Would you like a couple of extra tickets for your friends?"

"Yes, thanks," said Bronte, immediately thinking of how much Camille would love to go.

An uneasy silence fell across them as Bronte struggled for something to talk about: she couldn't face hearing any more about polo or horses, but those seemed to be the only two subjects Sebastian was capable of holding a conversation on. Eventually, she caved and asked him about his next polo session.

She was very glad to hear the sound of the echoing knocker a few minutes later. Sebastian led her once more through the old house, but this time left her at the front door, giving Ryan a stiff nod.

"Do you need anything from your car?" Ryan asked.

"No, I've got my handbag."

"OK, let's get you home, you look frozen," he said, noting her goosebumps and arm-hugging stance.

Opening the passenger door, Ryan ushered her in. He grabbed a blanket from the back seat and insisted she bundle herself up. She didn't resist being fussed over, acknowledging his kindness with a tired but heartfelt thanks. He put the heating on high as soon as he started the engine, and they drove away in silence. Bronte was extremely grateful for his understanding that she just needed a moment's quiet. Eventually, he asked, "Are you beginning to thaw now?"

"A bit, thanks."

"Just how cold was it in that place?"

"It was a bit chilly," she admitted.

"You'd think the upper classes would put the heating on for guests."

"It didn't help that I wasn't exactly dressed for the time of year."

"Hmm . . ." replied Ryan noncommittally.

"Would you like to come in for a hot chocolate?" asked Bronte as Ryan pulled up outside the cottages: it was the least she could offer having got him out at ten o'clock at night to rescue her.

"Great, but I'll make it," he said. "You go and get changed into something more comfortable."

"Are you sure?"

"Yep, I couldn't focus on my hot chocolate with you dressed like that anyway."

Bronte blushed, but before she said anything, he added, "I'd be too busy counting your goose pimples."

She laughed and opened the door. Running up the stairs, she narrowly avoided tripping over a hissing Mr Darcy, who'd heard Ryan's voice and was emerging from the comfort of the bedroom, eager to say hello.

By the time she came down again, wearing several layers and feeling much better, the fire was lit and hot chocolate was being poured into mugs.

"Fancy a game?" said Ryan pointing to the Scrabble board he'd spotted.

She smiled. "Absolutely," she said, and they settled down to do battle at the kitchen table.

It didn't take Bronte long to realise that she was having a much better, and certainly more relaxed, Saturday night with Ryan than she'd had with Sebastian.

CHAPTER SEVEN

Bronte slept in late the next morning. She and Ryan had ended up playing Scrabble until gone two a.m.

She got up refreshed and determined to be positive. Yes, the dinner at Fenworth could have gone better, but perhaps part of it was her own fault for expecting too much. She should be thrilled that Sebastian wanted to include her in a family dinner, and she was sure Lord and Lady Fairfax would become friendlier over time. Their apparent rudeness could well have been down to their own nerves at meeting her, combined with a natural upper-class reserve. And certainly the house was cold, but it was a large building in the middle of winter, she should have been properly dressed for it.

She couldn't have made too terrible an impression if Sebastian wanted her to come to the ball as his date. She'd never been to a real ball before, despite writing about plenty, and couldn't wait . . . And presumably they'd have to turn the heating on for all those guests! She'd ring Camille later and see if she'd like to come; she'd promised to call anyway. Maybe Ryan would be interested as well. It would be fun to all go together.

Her phone beeped and she grinned as she read the message from Ryan:

How's the wounded pride? 3-2 I beat you!

Before she could answer, another message came through:

If you're looking for Mr Darcy he's fast asleep on my sofa. He turned up here at 6! Is this a plan to break me through lack of sleep so you have a chance at Scrabble victory?

Checking her back door, she could see Mr Darcy had managed to undo the clasp on the cat flap, which she'd closed last night.

Sorry! she texted back, *Shall I come and get him?*

I'll bring him back. Fancy a pub lunch? came the reply.

Sure, ready in 30 minutes?

See you then.

* * *

A little later, Mr Darcy had been returned home, much to his disgust, and Bronte and Ryan were in Ryan's car again heading off to the Swan. "I'd feel bad going anywhere else, they're so welcoming to my writers' group," explained Bronte.

"I don't mind where we eat as long as I get some Yorkshire puddings."

"I promise you they do very good Yorkshire puddings."

"Are you sure you don't mind roughing it at the local pub, after being wined and dined at Fenworth?"

"Oh, I think I'll cope."

Despite Ryan's obvious curiosity, Bronte hadn't told him much about what had gone on the evening before. This was partly because she'd feel guilty and like she was betraying Sebastian if she told Ryan how disappointing her time at Fenworth had been, but she was also rather embarrassed. She'd finally been swept off her feet by the perfect hero, rescued from genuine distress by a lord on horseback. Well, the son of a lord, but close enough. And they were actually dating! Only it wasn't turning out anything like she thought it would. For a start, she hardly saw him as he didn't seem keen to spend much time in the country. They also didn't appear to have very much in common. Their relationship, if that's what it could be called, was nothing like those in her books. But she knew she was being silly expecting real life to be like a romance novel. Sebastian was everything she wanted in a boyfriend, or at least she thought he was. It wasn't his fault the dinner had been a bit of a let-down, and she did have the ball to look forward to. What could be more romantic than being taken to a ball held in a beautiful stately home as the heir's date?

The pub was busy, with lots of locals choosing to spend their Sunday afternoon inside socialising on a rather miserable, drizzly day. They ordered two roast beefs with all the trimmings and sat down with their drinks.

There was a television in the corner and horse racing was on.

"Do you know much about horses?" Bronte asked.

"I can ride if that's what you mean. You?"

"No, not at all."

"Did you want to learn? I could teach you," Ryan replied.

"Maybe. Do you play polo?"

"Never tried it. Not much call for polo in a small Irish town."

I suppose I need to learn to ride before I learn to play polo, Bronte thought. And if I learn to ride, it might give me something to talk to Sebastian about.

"Do you really think you could teach me to ride a horse? I've never been on one before. Ever."

"Sure, it's not hard. One of the other dentists at the practice rides a fair bit, I'll speak to him if you like, find out where he goes and sort something out. Why the sudden interest?"

Bronte considered fibbing and saying it was something she'd been considering for a while, but decided honesty was the best policy, "Sebastian's really into horses and plays a lot of polo, it would be nice to understand what he's talking about!"

"Oh, right. Well, like I say, I can organise something."

"Great."

"Do you think your ankle's strong enough for it now?"

"I think so, as long as I start off slowly. It's almost completely better."

Their food arrived and they chatted away easily over their meal about their childhoods, comparing favourite toys and television programmes. They were both too full to manage a dessert, but craving something sweet on the way home, they popped into a supermarket to pick up some chocolates.

The rain was really pelting down by the time they got back. By unspoken agreement, they both went into Bronte's house. She was ignored by Mr Darcy, which made a nice change from being attacked by him. The cat walked straight over to Ryan, meowing, and was contentedly picked up and carried into the kitchen.

Bronte took off her coat and shoes in the hallway and called through, "How do you do that? He won't let me anywhere near him."

"Maybe he just prefers men."

"He didn't seem to think much of Sebastian."

Bronte thought she heard Ryan mutter something about "good taste," but was distracted by spotting an envelope she'd missed at the side of the door mat. Her name was handwritten on the front. Opening it, she found a short note from Sebastian, 'Tickets as promised. Will call when back from London.' There were three tickets to the ball, which was taking place in just under two weeks.

She brought them into the kitchen to sound out Ryan. He was making tea and absentmindedly stroking a purring Mr Darcy, who still lay in his arms.

"Sebastian's invited me to a ball at Fenworth. He's given me a couple of extra tickets, do you fancy coming?"

"And play third wheel to you and His Lordship? No thanks."

"I'm going to invite Camille. We can go as a group, it'll be fun."

"Perhaps . . ."

"There'll be free food and booze . . ." Bronte said, hoping Sebastian's mother wouldn't be in charge of the catering. "And it would be really nice to have someone to chat to if Sebastian gets drawn away by his polo friends."

"Alright then," Ryan conceded with a smile.

They spent the rest of the rainy afternoon playing Scrabble and watching Breakfast at Tiffany's. Bronte loved old films and this was one of her favourites. She adored the chemistry between Hepburn and Peppard, the music, the sparkling dialogue, just every magical moment of it; she couldn't believe Ryan hadn't seen it before. She was pleased he'd liked it, despite his initial dismissal of it as a 'bit of a girlie film.' Though he'd insisted that he choose the next film they watch together, She was anticipating plenty of guns. And possibly aliens.

Mr Darcy spent most of the film asleep on Ryan's lap. He was most unenthusiastic when his 'pillow' got up and prepared to leave. He attempted to sneak out with his friend, but Ryan picked him up and popped him back inside Bronte's house, "This is your home, matey. You stay here and look after your mistress." The cat did not look impressed.

Later, when she went upstairs to her bedroom, Mr Darcy was sat, seemingly waiting for her, at the turn in the narrow staircase. He purred as she approached, apparently pleased to see her.

"Night night, Mr Darcy," Bronte said as she passed him. He swiped at her leg, catching her trousers with his claw, but she was too fast for him to draw blood. Nasty, bad-tempered devil: his purr had clearly been a means of getting her to lower her guard.

If Holly Golightly's Cat had treated her like this, she'd have left him soaking wet in the alleyway and kissed Paul in the nice warm taxi, Bronte thought grumpily.

CHAPTER EIGHT

Ryan called round the following evening to talk about the riding lessons.

"I've booked you in for an hour's riding tomorrow evening at six. It's at the centre my colleague recommended, it's supposed to be a good class, and it's on every week, if you enjoy it."

"Um . . . my car won't be ready." She felt a little pathetic saying it, but it was true and, to be honest, she was feeling anxious about getting on a horse by herself and in two minds regarding the whole thing.

"I thought I could take you. If you want me to. Then you'd have someone there for moral support," he replied, reading her well.

"Would you really? I . . . I am a bit nervous."

"Don't worry: it's a beginners' group, and they'll put you on a really calm horse."

She took a deep breath. She could do this. "OK."

"I finish work about five thirty, so I'll drive straight home, get changed and take us both down."

"Thanks Ryan. You're a sweetheart. The garage picked up the car today, but said it'll be at least a week before it's fixed and ready to collect."

"Well, let me know if you need a lift anywhere else, or if you want anything picked up from the shops."

"I will," Bronte said gratefully, thankful for her kind neighbour.

* * *

As usual, Bronte turned to Camille for clothing advice in preparation for the class. She called her friend for an emergency shopping session the next morning. Naturally, Camille was more than happy to take charge, though Bronte did regret the invitation somewhat when it came to handing over her credit card in the equestrian store.

"Are you sure I need all this for just one lesson?" Bronte asked as they lugged her purchases to Camille's car.

"It's going to take more than one lesson for you to learn to ride Bronte, and you want to look the part. If you take yourself seriously, you'll take what you do seriously."

"That's a pretty good motto. Did you just make it up?"

"Yes, but quite fitting, no?"

"I suppose so," muttered Bronte, calculating whether or not she'd be able to afford heating for the rest of the month, or if she'd just have to wear her new riding kit under her usual clothes all the time in an effort to keep warm.

* * *

With Ryan due any minute to pick her up, Bronte gave herself a final once-over. She screwed up her face at her reflection: the black leather knee-high boots she wore were fine, she could pair those with jeans, and the white shirt was cute, but the breeches and show jacket seemed too much. She felt silly. She was considering taking her hair out of the French plait she'd managed to force it into, when she heard Ryan's knock at the door. Oh well, no time to change anything now.

Ryan struggled to keep a straight face when he saw her.

"Is there a problem?" she asked.

"You look like riding Barbie!"

"I'll take that as a compliment," she giggled.

"Did you really have all that riding gear in your house?"

"No, Camille took me shopping."

"I feel a bit of a mess next to you."

Ryan was in a pair of faded jeans, some battered boots and a thick jumper. His hair stuck up in tufts where he'd obviously changed in a hurry. Bronte felt an urge to reach up and smooth it down but stopped herself.

"At least you're not likely to be blinded by the glare from your own boots," she retorted.

"No danger of that."

* * *

Bronte had of course seen plenty of horses in fields since she'd moved here from London, but her sole experience of 'riding one' was when Sebastian had rescued her. The memory of that evening brought a blush to her cheeks. She hadn't paid that much attention to the actual riding of the horse then, she'd been more concerned with the pain coming from her ankle and Sebastian being so close to her. His strong arms had been a particular highlight, she recalled wistfully.

She felt tense and more than a little apprehensive as they arrived at the riding centre and found the reception.

"My, don't you look smart," said the woman taking Bronte's payment for the class, "We've given you Blossom. She's a lovely old girl, very placid and good-tempered, perfect for a novice. She's in stall four. If you make your way there, Nina will help you brush her and get her all saddled up."

That sounds promising thought Bronte.

They walked down a narrow, tree-lined lane to the stable block, passing several children preparing rather sweet little ponies ready to ride. One tiny girl, who looked about six years old, was already sitting confidently on her mount.

Stall four was easy to find: a large '4' emblazoned on its whitewashed walls and a hand-painted sign declaring

'Blossom' hung from the eves. A young woman, wearing a riding hat and carrying a saddle, saw them and called out, "I'll be with you in just a minute."

The top half of the door was open. Bronte sneaked a look inside and instinctively took a step back. The creature was huge. It must've been at least four times the size of the ponies she'd seen the children with! Just how heavy did they think she was to need something that big?! She'd never be able to even get up on this monster!

Sensing her panic, Ryan put his arm around her, "Don't worry, they said she's really gentle."

Hmm! Why am I thinking of Harry Potter and Hagrid's Care of Magical Creatures classes? Bronte thought. She was still considering making a run for the car when the woman in the riding hat reappeared, "Sorry for the wait, let's get Blossom kitted out for your ride."

Though a bit worried about the advice to watch out for the horse's back legs in case she decided to kick, Bronte quite enjoyed brushing her down: the horse ignored her, munching contentedly on hay. She felt a little self-conscious with Ryan there watching, but was glad he was around. He was very reassuring.

The saddle went on fine, but there was no way Bronte was going to put her hand anywhere near Blossom's mouth to put the bit in! She left that job firmly to Ryan.

Finally, Blossom was ready, and Bronte was instructed to lead her by the reins into the large arena where the lesson would take place. Luckily, Blossom was very tame and knew what was expected of her, because Bronte's nervous hold would have done absolutely nothing to stop the horse if she'd decided to wander off in a different direction.

In the sawdust-strewn arena, Bronte noted that everyone else in the class was under the age of ten and wore rather more pink than she did. They also didn't look like they were entering a show-jumping competition.

Bronte had taken so long faffing around with the reins that all the other riders were already on their horses. They seemed to turn as one to stare at her. A few mouths dropped open at her outfit. She looked over at Ryan, sat on a bench by the door. He gave her an encouraging smile.

Bronte gulped as the instructor asked her to get on Blossom and join the group. She felt everyone's eyes on her as she pulled a small mounting block over to the horse. Blossom waited stoically while she readied herself.

"Would you like some help over there?" called the instructor, a little impatiently Bronte felt: it wasn't that she was taking absolutely ages.

"I'm fine thanks!"

Bronte got on the step and clambered somewhat clumsily onto Blossom's back. She sat up straight and looked around her. She had actually managed to get on a horse by herself! Look how high she was! She glanced down and froze: she was very, very high. And not really very stable. Then Blossom seemed to get fed up of waiting for Bronte to sort herself out and began to trot towards the other horses. Not having put her feet in the stirrups, a bit shaky from nerves, and not expecting Blossom to move, Bronte slipped straight off the horse sideways and landed smack in the sawdust. Blossom stopped, sensing she no longer had a rider. Seeing Bronte on the floor, she gave a snort and walked calmly and with great dignity over to join her friends, wanting nothing to do with Bronte's ineptitude.

Bronte lay on the ground, too stunned to move. She'd landed hard on her right shoulder, and it hurt.

She heard, "Bronte! Are you alright?" and Ryan was suddenly by her side. He was immediately joined by the instructor who said desperately, "I did ask if she could manage!"

With a little help from Ryan, Bronte awkwardly sat up.

"I'm fine, I just banged my arm." Determination filled her, "I want to try again."

Didn't they say that if you fell off a horse it was essential you got straight back on? She wasn't going to let one little setback defeat her.

"Why don't you take a minute? You went down with quite a bang," said Ryan. "How's your ankle? Do you need me to carry you?"

"No, thanks, I can walk. My ankle's OK. Perhaps you're right — a little rest might be a good idea."

He helped her to her feet and over to the bench.

"Thank you for not laughing," Bronte said quietly.

"I'm warning you, I may have a chuckle about it later, but at the moment I'm still making sure you're OK."

They watched the children ride their horses round in a neat circle. They certainly made it look very easy.

"Just how did you do that?" asked Ryan finally. "I mean you just slipped right off its side. How?!"

"Natural ability, I guess."

Another couple of instructors had come into the arena. One took over the class while the woman who'd checked on Bronte went into a corner and talked urgently with the other. There were quite a lot of arm movements and the occasional look over at Bronte.

The pain in Bronte's shoulder had eased, and she got up. She was stubbornly resolved not to give in and to at least stay on a horse for the rest of the session.

"Good luck," said Ryan.

"I think I'm going to need it," Bronte replied.

She walked towards Blossom, who was now tethered to a gate, enjoying some water. She didn't get very far before the two instructors broke their rather agitated conversation and came rushing over to intercept her.

"How are you? Is your arm alright?" asked one.

"Yes, thank you, it's fine now. I'd like to try again."

"I'm afraid that won't be possible."

"Excuse me?"

"You could have done some damage to your shoulder, and to be honest I'm not sure it's a good idea for you to continue in case you fall off again."

"But I'm not planning on falling off again!" said Bronte desperately.

"We're really sorry. Of course, we won't charge you for the lesson, if you go to reception they'll give you a full refund."

Bronte was sure Blossom gave her a haughty glare.

"Come on, looks like we're going home," Bronte said, rejoining a surprised Ryan.

"Did you change your mind about getting back on? Has your shoulder started hurting again?"

"I'll explain later," she whispered.

They walked straight to the car. Bronte wasn't about to go and get her refund from reception, she'd be too embarrassed. She'd just have to chalk it up as a write-off. "They thought I shouldn't carry on with the lesson because of my shoulder and in case I fall off again," she said once they were in the car and well out of earshot of anyone from the riding school.

"What about the money you paid?"

"They said I could have a refund, but I just want to leave it." Seeing that Ryan was going to protest, she added, "I can't go and explain what happened to everyone in the office!"

"I'll deal with it," said Ryan, and before she could stop him he was marching towards the reception. Bronte put her head in her hands, what a nightmare!

He returned a few minutes later and wordlessly handed her the money.

"Thank you," she muttered. "Can we please just go home now?"

"Sure," he said, giving her a kind smile.

* * *

Bronte was still feeling sorry for herself two days later. She'd taken a break for lunch and was trying to get back into her writing. The story was flowing better now, but not going in the direction she wanted it to: her heroine seemed to be much happier spending time with her hero's brother than with the hero, who was coming across as rather boring and self-absorbed. Still, she'd persevere and get the first draft done and then fiddle with the characters to make it work later.

Deep in thought, she was surprised to hear her name called loudly from outside. And even more surprised on opening the door to find Ryan standing by her garden gate with two horses. He held a set of reins in each hand.

"Shouldn't you be at work?" Bronte asked mistrustfully.

"I took the afternoon off."

"Should I ask why you have those horses?"

"You wanted to learn to ride, I'm going to help you."

She opened her mouth to protest, but Ryan was resolute, "Get those riding boots of yours on, oh, and the hat. But please don't bother with the full gear, I can't face waiting out here with these two while you get changed. What you're wearing will be fine."

As commanded, Bronte grabbed her boots, hat and a coat, and joined him.

"This way, milady," Ryan said and he led the horses down the lane. They ambled along for maybe five minutes. Bronte enjoyed the clip-clop noise of the horses' hooves on the path, but warily made sure she kept well away from their mouths and hind legs.

They walked into a field, "I know the owner, he said he's more than happy for us to use it."

Bronte looked doubtfully at the horses and the large open space.

"Trust me. You'll be fine. Plus there's no one around so there's no need to feel self-conscious: if you do fall, which you won't, it'll only be me who sees."

Bronte wasn't convinced, and would cheerfully have turned right around and gone back home to her computer if it hadn't been for the amount of effort Ryan had clearly put into organising this for her. He was a really good friend, and she wasn't going to be ungrateful.

"OK," she said, "But if I fall off again I'm out of here!"

"Deal! But you won't fall off."

He tethered the larger of the two horses to the fence and led the other over to Bronte. "This is Gwendoline, and my horse is her brother, Horace. I have it on very good authority that she's extremely placid. I've got her all saddled up, ready for you. Here, lead her around a little." He handed her the reins.

Gwendoline was certainly a lot smaller than Blossom. She was white with brown patches and her forelock fell over her right eye, causing her to give an occasional little snort and a toss of her head. Bronte reached up and stroked her nose. "Try feeding her this," Ryan handed Bronte an apple. "Just put it in the palm of your hand and hold it out to her. She won't hurt you."

Bronte did as instructed, and the horse bent down and very gently took the whole apple into her mouth, leaving Bronte's hand a tad soggy but unscathed.

"I'll help you up and make sure you're all settled with your feet in the stirrups before I get on Horace, OK?"

"OK," agreed Bronte with a self-reassuring nod. She was going to do this.

Ryan cupped his hands and Bronte used them as a step and got on Gwendoline's back. She didn't feel nearly as high or precarious as she had in the brief time she was on Blossom. Ryan adjusted the stirrups before getting Bronte to put her feet in them and showed her how to properly hold the reins. Then he untethered his own horse and mounted. While she waited, Bronte kept almost painfully still, certain that if she made any sudden movement, Gwendoline would gallop off across the field, over fences and goodness only knows where. Her heart gave a little jump when the horse bent her head down to munch some grass.

"These two are best friends so they're happy to ride next to each other and I'll be right here beside you," said Ryan reassuringly.

They set off at a slow amble, the animals seemingly happy to take their time and not at all bothered by their riders. Swallowing the surge of panic that had flooded her with Gwendoline's first plodding step, Bronte struggled to time her awkward movement in the saddle with the unfamiliar rolling, lurching gait.

"If you pull gently on the reins either to the left or the right the horse will go that way. If you pull gently on both sides she'll stop."

Bronte nodded, focussing intently on gripping with her knees and holding onto the reins for dear life.

"If you want to go faster you squeeze with your legs. That will make Gwendoline go into a trot." Seeing the alarm on Bronte's face, Ryan quickly added, "But we won't do that today. Today we're just going for a few easy circuits of the field to get you both used to each other."

Bronte nodded again. As Ryan had said, the horses walked contentedly side by side. Bronte did tug hesitantly on the reins to turn when they reached the corners, but she soon saw she didn't really need to, Gwendoline knew what she was doing. Ryan kept up pleasant chatter about where he'd borrowed the horses from and what he knew about them, which helped with Bronte's nerves. A couple of turns about the field and she even began to feel her rigid grip on the reins beginning to loosen the tiniest bit.

After they'd been riding for about half an hour, they brought the horses back to the gate they'd entered by. Ryan dismounted first and then helped Bronte down.

"It's not far to their stables, only about a ten-minute walk. Do you want to help lead them back, or would you rather get straight back home?"

"I'll help," said Bronte. Her legs were quite wobbly, but they felt more like themselves after a few minutes walking.

Rambling along the maze of narrow high-hedged lanes, gently chivvying the horses along when they stopped to munch on a particularly tasty patch of verge, they soon reached a large, ivy-draped, stone farmhouse. Bronte recognised it at once from the view from her bedroom window. The rather weather-beaten farmer and his dogs met them in the yard.

"Thanks for the loan, John. This is Bronte, my friend I told you about," introduced Ryan, shaking the man's hand. "Gwendoline and Horace belong to John's son and daughter," he explained.

"Thank you for letting me ride her," said Bronte.

"No problem, you're actually doing me a favour," replied John, "With Fiona and Jack off at university now, I'm grateful to anybody who wants to take the horses out for a bit. What did you think of Gwendoline?"

"She was lovely, very patient with me!" said Bronte with a laugh.

"Shall I take them back to the stables?" Ryan asked.

"Just leave them with me, I'll let them out in the paddock for a bit as the weather's good."

John took the two sets of reins.

"Can I let you know if we'd like to take them out again?" said Ryan.

"Any time! You sorted that tooth of mine out, when no one else could fit me in for a week! Agony it was! Ride the horses whenever you like!"

They said goodbye and wandered back up the lane to their cottages.

"Thank you so much for that," said Bronte.

"No problem. Did you enjoy yourself?"

"I kind of did! I was very nervous, but it got better after a while."

"Do you think you'd like a second lesson?"

"That would be nice, but I want to do something to thank you."

"Well . . . now that you mention it, there is something you could . . ."

"Oh yeah," Bronte raised an eyebrow.

Ryan blushed slightly, "My family are coming over from Ireland to visit tomorrow. They're staying for the weekend. It'll be my mum, my dad and my little sister Caitlin. She's fifteen. I was wondering if you'd come round for supper with us tomorrow night? You being there might prevent my mum from spending the whole time cleaning the house." Realising he may not have sold the evening quite as well as he could, Ryan added, "I'm sure you'll like them."

"It's the least I can do, and it would be lovely to meet your family. Should I bring anything? Why don't I make pudding?"

"Are you sure that's alright?"

"Yep, of course."

"That would be brilliant. I've got the rest of today to shop and tidy but I'm working until four tomorrow, and they're due at the station at five, so I'll be a bit rushed."

"If you leave me a set of keys, I'll pop in and chuck the hoover around for you."

"You don't have to do that!"

"Honestly, I don't mind."

Ryan sighed with relief. "Thank you so much, you're a lifesaver."

* * *

Bronte spent the next morning making individual chocolate mousses. She didn't often make them, as it wasn't really worth it just for one; it was nice to have people to cook for today. The autumnal sun shone in the clear, pale blue sky. She enjoyed its warmth on her skin as she walked down into town to buy some fresh raspberries to serve with the mousses and a huge bunch of purple gladioli to brighten up Ryan's kitchen.

Letting herself into his cottage when she returned, she made an assessment of what needed doing. It certainly wasn't very tidy, despite all his obvious efforts from yesterday, but it was warm and homely. She made herself a cup of coffee and looked around, trying to imagine it through Ryan's parents' eyes. She started with the small pile of dirty dishes on the kitchen counter, giving a little smile at his cereal bowl which had the remains of his morning Frosties in the bottom. It seemed rather sweet that he ate kids' cereal. She wondered what Sebastian had for breakfast . . . probably something terribly manly involving kippers or kidneys, but cooked by 'Mummy' no doubt.

She gave the sides and the table a wipe down, then had a look in the cupboards for a vase, but with no luck: the closest thing was a pint glass. Men! Nipping into her own cottage to get one, she narrowly avoided being tripped up by Mr Darcy as she left again.

After arranging the flowers, Bronte went upstairs to see if there was anything she could do there. The two bedrooms and bathroom were all tidy, but the beds were unmade: Ryan must have stripped them earlier, ready for his family. She found the bed linen and made them up, then opened the windows to give the upstairs a bit of an airing. She hunted out clean towels and put them in the bathroom before putting a load of washing on and hoovering. How strange she thought: the mundane chores that she usually wasn't too keen on when doing them for herself became much more satisfying when she was doing them to help Ryan.

Once she'd finished, she went back home to get some writing done — her hero's brother, Douglas, was now helping Pippa plan a surprise party for Angus. Unfortunately, they seemed to be spending more time flirting than actually planning, and Bronte was struggling to keep them on message.

Bronte heard Ryan's car pull up outside just after four. A couple of minutes later a text came through on her mobile: *You're awesome. The place looks amazing.* She couldn't help grinning; it felt so good to do something nice for him, he was so appreciative. Ryan soon left again, presumably to pick his family up. Another half an hour went by before his return. Happy, cheerful voices carried on the air as he and his family walked up the path to his cottage. She couldn't make out what was being said, but the strong Irish accents were clear.

She worked for a little longer, subconsciously listening out for sounds telling her what was happening next door. She still found it peculiar to be able to hear so much of what went on. It would be awful if Ryan brought a woman home with him one night. Her stomach plummeted at the thought. She wondered why. They were just friends, she didn't have any sort of hold on him. She supposed it wouldn't be the same between them if he had a girlfriend. But she was seeing Sebastian, and it was only a matter of time until their relationship became more physical, so it wasn't fair to expect Ryan not to find someone of his own.

He'd been her neighbour for such a short time, but she liked having him around. Having a friend right there if she fancied a chat was great, that was all. Perhaps she was being a little bit selfish. Maybe she should make an effort to get Camille and Ryan together more, and see if something happened between them? She knew Camille fancied Ryan, but she hadn't noticed anything to suggest Ryan reciprocated. Which was actually quite odd: the glamorous Frenchwoman with her exotic accent invariably attracted plenty of male attention. An image of them together flashed in her mind. She shook her head to get rid of it.

Bronte went upstairs to change. She wouldn't usually bother if she was just popping across to see Ryan, but she wanted to make an effort as she knew his parents' visit meant a lot to him. She chose her best 'meeting the parents' outfit consisting of a fitted brown pencil skirt and a pale blue shirt. She added a cardigan to make her look more relaxed and put some earrings on. She brushed her hair and tied it back into a high ponytail and freshened her make-up.

She felt a little unsure of herself as she went down the stairs and into the kitchen. Sensing he was being deserted, Mr Darcy glared at her disdainfully from the kitchen table, which he was well aware he wasn't allowed to climb on. Judging by the little splashes of liquid around it, he'd also been helping himself to the cup of tea she'd left next to her laptop.

"Don't worry, I won't be late," she said. He turned his back on her.

Bronte grabbed the mousses and raspberries from the fridge and went next door. The front door was opened, before she'd even reached it, by a small, round woman. She looked in her late fifties and had the same red hair as Ryan. Her huge welcoming smile helped calm Bronte somewhat.

"Bronte, how lovely to meet you! We've heard so much about you!"

"No you haven't!" shouted out Ryan, "Mum, stop trying to embarrass me!"

"Alright!" Ryan's mother called back. "Maybe I haven't heard that much about you, but I'm very eager to. I'm Mary, Ryan's mum." The words came quickly with a thick brogue, and her warm smile never ceased to beam.

"Hello, it's lovely to meet you," said Bronte shyly.

"Well, come on in! What's that you've got with you? Has my lazy son got you bringing your own food when you're invited for tea?"

"Oh no, I offered! I wanted to bring something," Bronte said. She followed Mary into the kitchen, where the rest of the family were congregated.

"He'll be getting you to tidy up after him next!" said Mary.

Bronte caught Ryan's eye and gave him a little wink: she wouldn't reveal his secret.

"Though, I must say, his place does look nice. I'm impressed," continued Mary. "Now, this is my husband, Peter," she said, indicating a tall man with dark hair who stood by the sink.

"Nice to meet you, Bronte," he held out his hand. Bronte quickly put down the food she was carrying so she could shake it.

"And this is our daughter, Caitlin."

Caitlin took after her mother, with vibrant red hair, though Caitlin's was waist length and Mary's was cut in a bob. She was tapping away on a mobile phone, but looked up when her name was mentioned and gave Bronte a little wave.

"I apologise about Caitlin and that contraption. I'm hoping we'll be able to have it surgically removed at some point."

"Sorry, Mum!" Caitlin put the phone in her pocket. This was obviously a conversation they'd had a lot.

Ryan came over and kissed Bronte on the cheek, "Thanks for coming, and for pudding."

"It's a pleasure. I made chocolate mousse, I hope that's ok?"

"Definitely."

Ryan tried to shoo his family into the sitting room so he had space to lay the table, his dad and Caitlin went and put the television on, but Mary insisted on helping. Bronte liked hearing her fuss over her son, checking he'd been eating enough and not working too hard.

Ryan lifted the lid off the large saucepan simmering on the stove and gave the contents a stir. He had his hand swiftly bopped by a wooden spoon brandished by the chef.

"Paws off!" she said firmly.

"It smells amazing," said Bronte, "What are you cooking?"

"I was going to make a curry," replied Ryan, "I had everything in." He opened the fridge door to show her all the food. "But my dear mother decided she was cooking, so she's made coddle."

"Oh, don't be cross with me Ryan, it's been so long since I've cooked for you and you know how I like to."

"I know," said Ryan, giving his mum a hug, "Don't worry, I'm not really cross: I'm really looking forward to some of your cooking." Turning to Bronte he added, "Mum's even brought her homemade soda bread all the way from Ireland, to go with it. I'm not quite sure how she managed to fit any clothes in her suitcase, there was so much food in it, I think it's probably best not to ask."

Mary gave him another tap with the spoon and they all laughed. The atmosphere was so light and cheerful, it couldn't have been more different from her dinner with Sebastian's family.

Ryan's little table was laid, more chairs were borrowed from Bronte's house, and glasses of wine poured. It was a bit of a squeeze when everyone sat down, but no one minded. Mary served. Ryan didn't even bother fighting her for that right.

The food was delicious: the coddle full to bursting with sausages, bacon, potatoes, onions and fresh parsley, and the brown soda bread perfect for mopping up the gravy.

A huge bowl was ladled out for Bronte, which she didn't think she had any hope of finishing, but somehow she did, along with two thick slices of bread. She did have to turn down a second helping though, for fear the strain on her skirt button might cause it to pop off.

By unanimous vote, they decided to wait a while before attempting pudding. Ryan made them all mugs of strong tea to aid with their digestion, and they got the Scrabble board out. Apparently, Ryan had told his father that he and Bronte played, and Peter was keen to take her on.

Caitlin gave a suitably teenage roll of her eyes at the suggestion she join in and was pleased when Ryan pointed out there were five of them and Scrabble was a game for a maximum of four players. She happily settled down with her phone and the television.

Bronte was having a wonderful time: she adored playing board games, and the mood was so friendly yet everyone was extremely competitive. It was all perfect. She did her best against Peter, but ruefully had to acknowledge that her best just wasn't good enough. It was however good enough to pip Ryan, much to everyone's delight. She loved how well he took the amiable ribbing, how at ease with himself he was.

After the victory parade and the clearing of the wounded, Bronte brought out her chocolate mousses: each little ramekin surrounded with gorgeous juicy raspberries, all liberally dusted with icing sugar; and to her delight, everyone tore into them, with many compliments.

"Whoever marries you will be a very lucky man," said Mary, giving Ryan a rather pointed stare. Ryan looked terribly uncomfortable.

"So, you live next door? How long have you lived there? Do you live by yourself?" Peter asked Bronte, changing the subject.

"I moved in a couple of years ago and, yes, I live by myself."

"Don't you find it a bit creepy being all alone here in the middle of nowhere?" piped up Caitlin.

"No, not particularly!" replied Bronte with a laugh.

"I bet you're happier now you've got a strong, capable, young man close by," commented Mary.

"Definitely." Bronte caught Ryan's eye again as he cringed and gave him a smile.

Mary stifled a yawn.

"You're tired, Mum," said Ryan kindly.

"I am actually. Would you mind terribly if your dad and I went off to bed, love? It's been a long old day."

"No, of course not, just give me a holler if there's anything you need."

"Are you sure you'll be alright down here?" asked Mary, eyeing the tiny sofa sceptically.

"You're not honestly thinking of sleeping on that, are you? You'll only be able to fit half of you on it," said Bronte.

"It's only for a couple of nights. I'll be fine."

"Why doesn't Caitlin sleep there?" suggested Mary. "She's much smaller than you."

"That's fine with me," said Caitlin.

"But then we'll all disturb you when we get up in the morning," said Ryan. "I understand as a teenager you can't be expected to get up before ten at the weekend."

"Why don't you sleep in my spare room?" suggested Bronte. "It's only a single bed, but it's certainly longer than your sofa. It won't take me a minute to get it ready for you."

Bronte saw Mary and Peter exchange a knowing look behind their son's back. She decided to ignore it.

"That would be great," said Ryan, gratefully.

They finished the clearing up and made sure Ryan's family had everything they needed, then left together.

Bronte found she was a little awkward now it was just the two of them, which was silly as they'd been in similar situations many times before and she'd felt perfectly comfortable then.

"Um, would you like a glass of water for the night?" she asked.

"Thanks, yes."

"You can use the bathroom first if you want."

"Sure, I'll go up now."

"Your room's the one on the right. There are clean towels in the cupboard."

"Great."

Bronte heard the stairs groan a little under his weight as Ryan went up, then the gentle padding of Mr Darcy's paws shadowing his friend. She locked the doors and windows and went upstairs. She heard water running in the bathroom as she made up the bed in the spare room. The bathroom door opened just as Bronte had finished the bed, and Ryan came into the bedroom wearing just a pair of pyjama bottoms, his chest bare.

Bronte gulped. She hadn't expected a dentist's torso to be quite so muscly and toned.

"Bed's all done!" she said overly-cheerfully.

"Thanks. Can I um . . . just get my t-shirt," Ryan asked, pointing to a grey clump of material Bronte was inadvertently standing on.

"Of course, sorry!" she replied, moving aside.

He picked up the top. Bronte couldn't help watching him as he bent down, his strong back muscles flexing, but she averted her gaze as he stood up again.

"Well, sleep tight, then," she said quietly, doing her best to keep her eyes off his semi-naked body. She quickly skirted around him, rushed into the bathroom herself, and shut the door firmly. Blimey! What was going on with her? That definitely wasn't the sort of reaction you had to someone who was 'just a friend.' She decided she must be missing Sebastian. She hadn't had a boyfriend for a long time, and now look at the state she'd gotten herself into, lusting after anything male, she thought, doing her best to find the humour in the situation.

Bronte went to sleep, planning to call Sebastian in the morning. Maybe she could go to London and have dinner with him. Perhaps she could even stay the night with Sebastian in his London house. Though actually, come to think of it, his parents would probably be there, and she wasn't sure she could handle another evening with them. At least not so soon. She and Sebastian could go to a lovely hotel instead. She'd always wanted to stay at Claridge's. They could have champagne and strawberries delivered to the room. It would be amazing . . . Then again, she'd better check her bank balance before she made too many elaborate plans!

* * *

A loud crash followed by a thud woke Bronte. Heart racing and mind all foggy, she looked across at her bedside clock: it was just after one in the morning.

She climbed hurriedly out of bed to investigate the noise. As far as she'd been able to tell, the racket had come from inside the house. Well, she couldn't imagine any burglar in his right mind traipsing all the way out here to her tiny cottage, but she needed to check. She'd only call Ryan if she really needed him. There was a chance he slept half-dressed, and she wasn't sure she could handle seeing his chest twice in one night.

Grabbing her hairdryer, the closest thing to a weapon she could quickly find, she crept out of her room and was greeted by more bangs. They were coming from the room across the hallway, the room Ryan was sleeping in. She knocked tentatively on the door. "Is everything alright?" she whispered, although she didn't know quite who she was being quiet for, there was no way Ryan could still be sleeping through that.

"Not really!" came the reply.

Ryan opened his door. Bronte noticed with relief that he was wearing his t-shirt. He stood back to let Bronte survey the damage. "Oh my!" she said, and burst out laughing.

The guest bed had completely collapsed. The struts supporting the mattress had given out under the weight of Ryan lying on them. The mattress itself had fallen straight through the hole and the ends of the bed must have then buckled in on themselves. The nightstand had been knocked over, which in turn, like well-placed dominoes, had toppled a small bookcase. Books, lamps, oddments and assorted debris lay scattered everywhere.

"Are you hurt?" she managed to ask.

"Only my pride," said Ryan, who was also laughing at the absurdity of the situation. "I don't think Mr Darcy is too impressed."

The cat was crouched in a corner, hissing crossly. He glared at Bronte. She was sure he blamed her completely. She moved forward to comfort him, but the hissing just increased and his front paw rose to swipe, so she thought better of it and backed away again.

"I'm so sorry!" Bronte said. "I bought the bed at an antiques auction a couple of months ago. It looked sound, but no one has actually slept in it since I got it."

"I don't think I can do anything to fix it right now — I'll unbury the mattress and sleep on the floor," Ryan replied.

"I don't think they'll be enough room. It's a pretty tight squeeze in here."

"I could drag it downstairs into the sitting room," he suggested.

"Look, why don't you just join me in my bed?" said Bronte before she could think better of it. "There's plenty of room and I promise I don't snore."

"Are you sure?" Ryan asked.

"Of course, why shouldn't I be?"

"Well, Sebastian might not be too impressed."

"Sebastian and I have only been on a couple of dates, it's no business of his if a friend sleeps in my bed. Anyway, there's nothing wrong with two friends sharing a big double bed. We're both adults and perfectly capable of keeping our hands to ourselves."

"I am, but I'm not so sure about you. Are you certain you'll be able to handle lying so close to this?" he said, pulling absurd bodybuilder poses, "And not being able to cop a feel?"

"I'll manage," Bronte laughed, although her heart was fluttering like crazy, and she wasn't too convinced of how strong her resolve would be if put to the test.

"Come on," she said, trying to sound confident, and led the way into her bedroom.

Ryan took in the room with interest; he hadn't seen it before. "Very pretty," he declared.

"Thank you. I sleep on the right-hand side, are you alright taking the left?"

"No problem."

They got into bed, both being very careful not to touch the other and to keep strictly to their own half of the bed.

There was a scratching at the door and a very sad "meow?"

"Oh for goodness sake," muttered Bronte under her breath. She got up and let the cat in. He promptly hissed at her, dodged her attempted pat and jumped onto the bed, settling himself down by Ryan's feet. She got back under the covers.

"Goodnight, Bronte," came Ryan's voice from the darkness.

"Goodnight, Ryan. Goodnight, Mr Darcy."

"Hiss!"

Silence reigned for a few seconds before Ryan asked, "By the way, what were you doing with that hairdryer?"

"Protection."

"Against me?!"

"In case the ruckus you made destroying my furniture turned out to be armed bandits."

"I'm sure your hairdryer would have sent them running for the hills," he teased.

CHAPTER NINE

In the flurry of emotions at having Ryan in her bed, Bronte thought it would take her ages to get to sleep, but actually it didn't. In only a few minutes Ryan's breathing had become low and even, and as Bronte listened she felt her eyelids grow heavy and soon she too was fast asleep.

She woke early before Ryan. Sitting up, she had a moment of sleepy confusion as to who was beside her before the mists cleared and it all came back. She couldn't help but give a little smile at the sight of him, sleeping there so peacefully, with the duvet pulled right up, so only his hair could really be seen. It looked soft and somehow inviting, and Bronte felt an urge to stroke it.

Bewildered, she quickly got to her feet. Any romantic feelings she might have been having about him rapidly vanished when she saw that, bizarrely, his dirty socks had ended up right in the middle of her bedroom floor. "Typical male," she murmured, kicking them out of the way as she headed to the bathroom.

She showered, humming contentedly. Over the previous evening's dinner, Ryan had invited her to join him and his family for the day and she'd jumped at the chance. They were going out to explore the local sites, most of which she somehow hadn't got round to visiting: she'd had great plans to take them all in when she'd moved to the area, but had never seemed to have the time, had always been too busy. So, she was looking forward to being a tourist for the day.

Wrapping a fluffy towel about herself, she sighed when she realised she hadn't brought her clothes in with her. Slipping quietly back into the bedroom so not to disturb Ryan, intending to grab what she needed then retreat to dress in private, she needn't have worried: the bed was empty. She felt oddly disappointed, a bit like her one-night stand had scarpered without even leaving his number. He'd just gone home of course. She'd see him again soon enough. He probably wanted to use his own shower. Maybe he was anxious to get back to his own family and make the most of the short time he had with them. She hoped he didn't regret asking her to join them on their day out.

She quickly got dressed in skinny jeans and a shirt, with a soft wool jumper over the top. It was a cold day so she needed to wrap up, plus there'd be a lot of walking, but she still wanted to look nice.

Putting on her make-up, she remembered she'd been going to give Sebastian a call to see if he'd like her to visit him in London — maybe she should just send a text now as it was still before eight. Her mobile was downstairs, so she'd text after breakfast.

She left her hair loose: she'd let it dry naturally for a bit while she ate and then finish it off with the hairdryer before venturing out.

She opened the bedroom door and a delicious waft of bacon hit her. Hurrying downstairs, she found her missing house-guest in her kitchen, plating up two enormous bacon sandwiches.

"Ah, perfect timing. I was just going to give you a shout," he handed Bronte a cup of tea.

"I thought you'd gone," she said.

"And left without saying goodbye after spending the night in your bed? That wouldn't have been very gentlemanly behaviour, now would it?" Bronte blushed.

"Where did you get the bacon from?" she asked. "I didn't have any. And this bread isn't mine."

"No, you only had that awful, thin, multi-seed stuff. I launched a raid on my own cupboards. No one was up over there so I grabbed the food and legged it."

"Are you sure you wouldn't rather be having breakfast with your family?"

"Nah, they're still asleep and I'm starving. Plus, Caitlin's awful first thing, she's best avoided until she's been up at least an hour. I showed them where everything was last night, so they could sort out their own breakfast whenever they got up. Oh, I did leave a note saying we'd see them around ten thirty, if that's OK?

"Fab," Bronte replied, between mouthfuls. "You make the most amazing bacon sandwiches."

"Yes, I do. The secret's in the bread. It has to be thick, soft and white. And smothered in proper butter. Anyway, eat up: if you like we can get a bit of a ride in before we meet up with that lot next door."

"Um . . . Alright — I guess we need to keep up the momentum. Shall I wear my riding jacket?" she teased.

"Maybe not, eh? We'll go down to the field again, but this time why don't we ride there from the stables rather than walking the horses?"

"On the roads?"

"Don't worry, they're only little country lanes. You'll be fine. I'll go in the front and lead the way."

"OK . . . I'll be brave."

"I tell you what, if you don't have a good time, I'll buy you the biggest slice of cake you can find. We're sure to stop in a coffee shop somewhere, my mum can sniff them out, it's like her superpower."

"Deal!" Bronte agreed happily.

* * *

It was very cold outside, but the brisk march to the farm well and truly woke Bronte up and brought colour to her cheeks.

She'd remembered to bring an apple for Gwendoline, who stuck her head out over the top of her stable door to greet them. Bronte held the fruit out in the palm of her hand and Gwendoline took it gently, giving a little whinny of thanks. Bronte stroked the horse's nose. She was definitely feeling more relaxed around her today.

She helped Ryan get the animals ready for their ride, though she quietly made sure he did anything that involved going round the back of them or putting stuff in their mouths. Ryan held Gwendoline's bridle as Bronte climbed up and made herself comfortable.

Ryan got on Horace and set off out of the stable yard and through the farmyard gate. With a very deep breath and a nervous look at the hard concrete, Bronte gave a gentle nudge with her heels, and they too were off. Ryan was waiting to close the gate after her, and within moments, their little procession was on its way along the path. As he'd promised, Ryan led, looking over his shoulder frequently to check Bronte was alright. She gave him a smile whenever she spotted this, but rather a tight one, as she was concentrating so fiercely on what she and her horse were doing. But Gwendoline was clearly fond of Horace and was happy to amble along behind him.

They got to the field and again Ryan dismounted and sorted out the gate. They started working their way around the perimeter as they had before, at a slow, leisurely amble. Bronte was beginning to unwind slightly and find a comfortable seat, when Gwendoline decided to bend her head down suddenly to munch on a particularly yummy looking piece of grass. Bronte gave a sharp squeal of alarm, which she did her best to stifle as soon as she realised she wasn't in any real danger. She suspected Ryan had heard but decided it best not to comment.

After a couple of circuits they stopped. "You doing OK?" Ryan asked. "Saddle comfy? Stirrups the right length?"

"I think so."

"Are you feeling crazy enough to trot?"

Bronte looked doubtful.

"Come on, live a little! Remember, if you have a bad time, that huge, gooey slice of cake is yours."

"Alright, I'll try it," she laughed.

"Great, we'll begin with the horses walking next to each other, then when Horace starts trotting, use your legs to give Gwendoline a squeeze and she'll also move into a trot. We'll only do a tiny bit: when Horace falls back to walking again, give a pull on the reins and Gwendoline will do the same," explained Ryan. "It'll be a bit bouncy, it helps if you try to raise your bottom off out of the saddle in time with the bumps."

"I need to synchronise stuff now?" asked Bronte, in despair, "I can't even walk and chew gum at the same time!"

"Don't worry, it sounds harder than it is."

"I'll take your word for it."

"Come on, let's get started, you're overthinking things." He made a clicking noise with his tongue and Horace lurched into motion. Bronte gave a gentle squeeze with her legs and Gwendoline again followed his lead. Then Ryan got Horace trotting and gave her a thumbs up. Taking another deep breath, Bronte gave a second squeeze. Her nerves meant it wasn't particularly strong, but the horse knew what to do. Bronte clung on so tightly her knuckles were white. She was tossed up and down like a boat in a storm until she recalled what Ryan had said, and finding the rhythm in her horse's gait, she attempted to move in time with it, which at least took her mind a little off how terrified she was.

Horace slowed to a walk and so did Gwendoline even before Bronte had gathered herself together enough to remember to pull on the reins.

"What did you think?" asked Ryan.

"Petrifying!" said Bronte, then added, "But actually kind of exciting."

They practised trotting three more times before setting off back to the stables. It was still pretty scary, but definitely more fun the more Bronte got used to it.

"Thanks for that," she said as they approached the farm.

"My pleasure. Did you enjoy yourself?"

"I did. You've saved yourself a piece of cake, mister."

Ryan smiled. "Excellent. My evil plan worked."

"You really will do anything to save a couple of pounds won't you?"

"Yep," he laughed.

Drawing to a halt in the deserted yard, they took the saddles and bridles off and gave the horses a rub down before letting them loose in the paddock. Walking back to the cottages, Bronte decided to quickly slip into her own house to tidy herself and grab her bag and mobile. Ryan came with her so he could pick up the bits he'd brought over for the night, then they joined his family and were ready to set off.

"Did you sleep well?" Mary asked her son.

"Not to begin with, the bed broke."

Mary's eyebrows shot up in surprise, "Goodness," she proclaimed.

Oh dear, thought Bronte, this could be rather misconstrued.

"It was a single bed, an antique," she added hastily, "I hadn't tried it out before." The eyebrows rose further. Oops! She really wasn't improving things at all she realised and decided to keep quiet.

They all managed to cram into Ryan's car with Bronte squeezing into the back with Caitlin and Peter. Caitlin was quieter this morning, but Bronte drew her out, asking her about her school and her friends, and the teenager became more confident as she talked.

She also asked Peter about his practice. It was interesting to hear it really seemed to be part of the fabric of his local community, there were people who now brought their kids to him, who'd been seen by Peter when they themselves were children. He'd even had the same receptionist since he'd opened the business almost thirty-five years before.

"Any chance you'll retire anytime soon, Dad?" called Ryan from the driver's seat.

"Any chance of you coming home and taking it over?" replied his father.

"Sorry, Dad, I'm happy where I am."

"Well, so am I."

The drive through the Kentish countryside was beautiful, even when the sky was overcast and threatened rain. The highlight was the thrill as she caught the first whiff of sea air and then spotted the Channel itself.

They'd all voted the night before to decide where they would explore. Caitlin had been very keen to go into London for the day, but they decided to save that for Sunday. Instead, they'd settled on Dover Castle as something they all fancied and which wouldn't require too long a drive. If the weather did stay fairly dry, they could venture down onto the beach for a stroll.

* * *

After a wonderful day, they got back to the cottages at six thirty. The castle had been fascinating and Ryan had been right about his mother's ability to track down good food: they'd had a delicious lunch in the castle's wartime-tunnels tearoom, then huge slabs of cake in a little café on the seafront. It had been the first time any of them had seen the White Cliffs of Dover.

It was only when she saw the tickets to the ball stuck on her fridge that Bronte remembered she'd planned to get in touch with Sebastian today. She'd just been having so much fun and been so relaxed with Ryan and his family, it had gone clean out of her mind.

As she wasn't sure what he'd be up to and hadn't left much time to organise something for the following day, Bronte thought it better to text than call. She typed, *Hi, How are things? Coming to London tomorrow, shall we meet up?* and pressed send. A response came through just a couple of minutes later saying: *Sounds good. Lunch at my club — The Lichen, Kensington. Wear a dress cut below knee. They're sticklers. 1 p.m.?*

See you then! Bronte replied, wondering to herself what sort of crazy club seriously only let women in if they were wearing a dress cut below the knee. Was he joking? She googled The Lichen and discovered it was an extremely old-fashioned gentlemen's club. Women weren't permitted to become members, but they were allowed to enter the bar and restaurant if chaperoned by a member. How decent of them!

Bronte had to admit she was more than a little intrigued, she'd never been anywhere like that before. She guessed she'd better search out her most respectable frock. And sort out her rather ratty-looking nails. And probably polish her shoes. Oh, and find some unladdered tights.

She had half an hour before she needed to be back next door again to join Ryan and his family for dinner, so she quickly ran around getting herself ready for the next day.

They ate supper in The White Swan, "It's the closest I've got to a local," explained Ryan.

"Are you looking forward to going into London tomorrow?" Bronte asked Caitlin.

"So excited! I'm heading straight to Top Shop and then Miss Selfridge. Then we're going to afternoon tea at The Ritz."

"Yes, I get to check out the latest purple eyeshadows and strappy vests," said Ryan.

"You're a very good big brother," said Bronte.

"I know. Truth is, I don't want her wandering around London by herself. I'm the teeniest bit over-protective."

"I think it's nice," said Bronte.

"I think it's annoying," said Caitlin.

"I know you've already given up loads of your time over the last couple of days, but do you fancy coming to trawl the shops with Caitlin and me tomorrow? Mum and Dad are going off gallivanting by themselves for a few hours and I promised to take her wherever she wants. She'll have much more fun with you there, and so will I."

"I'd love to, but I'm meeting Sebastian for lunch at one. I can travel in with you though, and support you through Top Shop at least."

"Who's Sebastian?" asked Caitlin.

"Bronte's boyfriend," Ryan answered quickly.

"I didn't know you had a boyfriend," said Caitlin, addressing Bronte.

"Well, it's quite new . . ." began Bronte.

"Can't you come for tea with us as well?" pleaded Caitlin, "It's going to be so posh."

"Sorry, I'd love to, but I'm not sure what Sebastian and I will be doing."

"It won't take you long just to eat lunch."

"Caitlin, leave it," Ryan looked embarrassed.

"Fine!" said Caitlin, and turned to talk to her mother.

"Sorry about that," whispered Ryan.

"Don't worry about it. Are you sleeping in my house again tonight?"

"Are you propositioning me, Ms Huntington?"

"Certainly not, Mr Murphy," said Bronte, feigning shock.

"Oh well, never mind, I'll still stay over."

* * *

"You're very dressed up," said Ryan, when Bronte came downstairs for breakfast the next morning.

"I suppose I am."

"I take it this is all for Sebastian's benefit," he said indicating her outfit.

"That and the fact that I have to wear a dress to get into the club he's taking me to for lunch."

"Do places like that really still exist?"

"That's what I wondered, but apparently so. Anyway, it's nice to dress up a bit when you're going somewhere special isn't it?" she added hastily, "Look at you, all smart for The Ritz, that's not really any different," she said, indicating the pressed shirt and trousers Ryan had on, and the suit jacket hanging on the kitchen chair.

"Women can wear trousers in The Ritz."

"There's nothing wrong with a bit of tradition," said Bronte, beginning to feel defensive.

"Of course not," said Ryan, realising he was perhaps overstepping the mark, "Sebastian's very lucky to have someone looking so lovely meeting him for lunch."

Bronte smiled. "That's more like it!" Any crossness, or worry that maybe Ryan was right, evaporated from her mind.

They collected their things together, ready to leave, and Bronte found herself watching Ryan's arms stretch as he put his suit jacket on. He must work out a lot to have muscles like that, she thought to herself idly, then tore her eyes away, worried he'd catch her gawping at him.

* * *

When they went over to Ryan's place they were amused to find Caitlin attempting to hurry her parents and chivvy them out.

"What's the panic?" asked Peter, mock-grumpily, "I thought we were supposed to be on holiday. Hi there son, fancy hanging around here for a couple of hours? Maybe we could do some gardening? There's no rush to get to London is there?"

"Oh no Dad, no rush at all. In fact, I'm wondering whether we actually want to bother going at all," replied Ryan, grinning and checking his little sister's reaction.

"Mum!" wailed Caitlin.

"Stop teasing the girl you two. We're leaving now Caitlin," said Mary, "You know they're only trying to wind you up."

Ryan and his father were still laughing about their joke as they all piled into the car. They drove to the station, having decided to save themselves a lot of hassle with parking and take the train into the city.

In the warmth of the train carriage, Bronte took her coat off.

"Oh, you look very nice," commented Mary.

"Thanks."

"Where's your boyfriend taking you?" asked Caitlin a little sullenly. She clearly didn't like the idea of Bronte having a beau.

"He's a member of a club and I'm meeting him there for lunch."

"Well, I bet it won't be as good as our tea at The Ritz."

Bronte laughed. "I'm sure it won't be."

The train took them to Charing Cross Station, where they got on the Underground to Oxford Circus.

"Wow!" exclaimed Caitlin as they stepped out into the daylight and the busy craziness of the London streets. "This is seriously awesome!"

"Caitlin and I are gonna hit the cool, hip shops," said Ryan, "Are you sure you two will be alright by yourselves?" he asked his parents.

It was sweet to see him fussing over them, thought Bronte.

"We'll be fine!" said Mary. "Your father and I will go to Liberty and wander about. We can all meet back here at two, and then move on to the Tate Modern before we head to The Ritz."

Mary and Peter disappeared into the crowds, and Caitlin dragged Ryan, closely followed by Bronte, into the famous flagship Top Shop store. Caitlin was in her element, and it was lovely to see Ryan doing his best to show an interest. His main job was to carry everything Caitlin grabbed to try on.

Caitlin had saved all her birthday and pocket money ready for this great event and planned to spend every penny of it.

Finally, after almost an hour and a half of walking around the huge store's three floors, Caitlin had narrowed her finds down to what she wanted and, much more taxingly, to what was actually within her budget. She dolefully put a pair of knee-high boots she couldn't afford back on the shelves, and Ryan conveyed her goodies to the check-out.

Once she'd paid, they finally escaped the manic store. Bronte and Ryan tried to make the most of the freshish air before they went to another shop.

Despite the shops not being much to Bronte's taste, she was having a lovely time, and even managed to pick up some jeans for herself. But all too soon she had to leave. "Just you and me now, kid," Ryan joked to Caitlin.

Bronte walked quickly back to the Underground station, checking her watch as she went. She'd left a bit later than she'd meant to: she'd just been having so much fun.

She was in luck, the train arrived quickly, and she made up some of her lost time. She changed at Piccadilly Circus, and in a few minutes had arrived at South Kensington. It took her a moment to get her bearings, but it wasn't long before she was at the road Sebastian's club was on. After twenty metres or so she reached her destination. The building was discrete but imposing: the architecture was pure Georgian, stucco walls, wrought-iron railings, high windows, all exuding exclusive elegance. 'The Lichen' was etched into the gleaming brass plaque next to the portico.

Ascending the grand steps, one of the large dark-green double doors opened at her approach and a stern uniformed doorman ushered her into the entrance hall. It really was like travelling back a hundred years. The walls were wood-panelled and adorned with portraits of enormous, pompous-looking gentlemen. A suit of armour stood rather precariously in one corner, and stags' heads glared from above with their glassy eyes.

The rumble of subdued chatter distantly carried from a corridor to the right, and on her left was an open doorway. Bronte peeped into a grand high-ceilinged room. It was full of large wing-backed chairs and there was a roaring fire at the far end. Most of the chairs were occupied by expensively-suited men immersed in their newspapers. It was so quiet, Bronte could hear the fire crackling from where she stood.

She'd become so engrossed in observing her surroundings that a polite cough from behind startled her so much that she jumped. She turned around and came face to face with another dour attendant; she must have walked straight past him on her way in. "May I help you, Miss?" he asked, looking her up and down. Presumably she passed his inspection because when she explained who she was here to see, he lost no time in instructing a footman, who'd silently manifested himself from somewhere, to take her through to dine. Following him along the opulently decorated corridor, she was finally passed over to a waiter, just as long-faced as the rest of the staff she'd met, in the dining room.

He sat her at a table for two by a window overlooking a pretty courtyard.

"Mr Fairfax hasn't arrived yet, but this is his usual table. Would you care to see the drinks menu?"

"Um, yes, please," said Bronte. The waiter handed her the heavy leather-bound tome and left. Bronte was then faced with the problem of deciding what to go for without knowing what Sebastian would fancy: she didn't want to order wine and then have him drinking only water, but neither did she want to choose a soft drink and then find him ordering something alcoholic. The memory of how he downed his 'snifters' when she went for dinner at Fenworth decided things: anyone who could hold that much liquor in an evening would never sip a glass of Coca-Cola with lunch. She opted for a glass of Chablis and a jug of iced water.

Fifteen minutes later, Sebastian still hadn't arrived and Bronte was beginning to regret not bringing a book or even her usual writing pad and pen to jot down some notes about this place: it would make a fantastic setting for a scene.

After half an hour Bronte was getting pretty annoyed. The waiter had been back twice to see if she needed anything, and it was embarrassing. She'd tried to call Sebastian, but his mobile just went to voicemail and she didn't have his home number in London. She was about to get up and leave when the man himself came into the room. He flashed her a smile and put his hand up in greeting, then wove his way through the other tables to where she sat. Stopping frequently to talk to various, mostly quite elderly men, presumably friends of his father's, he finally sat down opposite Bronte.

"Hello there! I'm famished. Have you decided what you're having? The lamb is terribly good, almost as nice as Mummy's." Bronte immediately resolved to avoid the lamb.

"No, I haven't looked at the food, I was waiting for you."

"Oh, I hope you weren't waiting long," he said absent-mindedly as he signalled to the waiter for some menus and a drink.

"Not at all," said Bronte, gritting her teeth, not wanting to start an argument which would spoil the lovely afternoon she still hoped they'd have.

The menus and an obscenely large whiskey were swiftly brought over.

Bronte read through the choices, hiding a smile that everything was rather old-fashioned, comforting nursery food. It was just what the members' nannies would have made for them on a cold winter's evening before dressing them in their thick flannel pyjamas (to keep out the chill running through the corridors of their huge old houses) and presenting them to Mummy and Daddy for a goodnight kiss, or a telling off if they'd warranted it.

Something that had been vaguely nagging at the back of her mind suddenly resolved and she realised that the room smelt of the school dinners of her childhood: all overcooked meat and tinned vegetables.

She chose roast chicken with vegetables and gravy, which seemed like a fairly safe option. Sebastian went for his favourite lamb chops. He smacked his lips with excitement when the waiter brought them over. It did indeed look remarkably similar to something his mother would have produced.

Bronte worked her way methodically through her rather bland meal while Sebastian talked about what he'd been doing in London, the parties he'd been to and the inevitable polo practices he'd taken part in.

He was certainly very handsome, and it wasn't any hardship to watch him while he chatted away, but it occurred to Bronte that he acted almost like a small child: he had next to no responsibilities and barely seemed to think about anything that didn't directly affect him. It didn't occur to him to ask Bronte why she'd come into London, or even how her work was going, and in the end, she decided it would be too much effort to interrupt the flow of his conversation to try to say anything about herself.

They finished their main courses, and the waiter appeared to clear away their plates and bring them the dessert menu. Bronte wasn't surprised to find it included Eton Mess, Spotted Dick and Jam Roly-Poly. She contemplated ordering something, mainly so she'd be able to regale Ryan with how awful it had been after he'd filled her in with all the delights he'd enjoyed at The Ritz, but changed her mind when Sebastian declared he'd just have a quick espresso.

Sebastian downed his coffee as soon as it arrived. "Well, I'd better get going," he said, getting up, "Mummy and Daddy are having a late luncheon and made me promise I'd show my face. Don't want them cutting off the old allowance again! Err . . . can you just have this stuck on their account actually? I really can't be late."

Before she had a chance to answer, he'd given her a fleeting peck on the lips and was gone.

Feeling totally dejected, Bronte checked her watch: it wasn't three yet. If she went home now she could get some writing in, she reflected despondently. But she wasn't in a particularly romantic sort of mood anymore and the prose would end up reflecting that. Ryan and his family had their table booked in The Ritz's Palm Court for four . . . it wouldn't take long to get to Green Park by tube, and then she'd be practically at the hotel. She could easily be there in time to meet them. Would it be an imposition? Caitlin had invited her after all. Their company would be just the tonic to pick up her spirits. She quickly texted Ryan to ask if it was alright for her to gate-crash their tea, and he replied straight away to say they'd all be delighted if she would.

Finishing her coffee, Bronte charged the meal to Sebastian's parents. She felt terrible for doing so but didn't really know what else to do without causing offence. They didn't even bring a bill over, the waiter just nodded gravely when Sebastian's request was explained. She imagined the prices there would be pretty hefty.

She was terribly disappointed about how things had gone with Sebastian. He'd been so late, even though he knew she'd be waiting for him somewhere she hadn't been before and might not feel completely comfortable in. And then he'd only given her just over an hour of his time! Though to be fair, he'd never said he was free for more than that, and just imagine if he'd suggested she join him for the afternoon with his parents and their cronies? How would she have got out of that one? But it would've been nice to have felt that Sebastian actually wanted to spend more time with her.

She also didn't like that he'd used his parents' account to pay for their meal, or his casual mention of the allowance they paid him. Neither of these fitted with the image of him in her head. In fact, she was rapidly coming to suspect her fictitious image was just that, and it didn't quite match the real Sebastian Fairfax at all.

* * *

Bronte arrived at The Ritz as it was just approaching four and saw Ryan waiting outside.

"Hiya!" she said, "How did the rest of the shopping go?"

"Pretty well. I am now an expert in orange nail varnish and I'm in Caitlin's good books since I bought her those boots she liked in Top Shop."

"Soft touch."

"I know, but I don't get to spoil her often. So, how come you're finished with Sebastian so early?"

"Oh, he had things he needed to do," said Bronte honestly, but quickly changed the subject before Ryan could enquire further, "Are you sure it's alright for me to join you?"

"Of course, everyone's thrilled. I think they may even prefer you to me, which is a little galling. To tell you the truth, my mum organised this a while ago and had booked for five people anyway, hoping I'd bring a girlfriend."

"Lucky for me you didn't, eh?" Bronte grinned, linking arms with him.

"I'm just hoping you're still too full after your lunch to be able to manage much, so I can have your leftovers. I've heard they won't let you have a doggy bag, so every crumb needs to be eaten from those silver platters!"

"Sorry to disappoint, but I only had one course and I've got plenty of room left for sandwiches and cake, you've got no chance of getting any of mine!"

CHAPTER TEN

Bronte and Ryan were up early the next morning. He'd stayed the night in her house again, but in the guest room on the mattress, after the bits of broken bed had been cleared away. Bronte was choosing to ignore the fact she'd slept better when they'd shared a bed, deciding to put it down to coincidence.

Ryan's family's train was leaving at 8.30 a.m., and Bronte had said she'd come to the station to say farewell.

Mary and Peter hugged their son tightly as they said goodbye. "Don't go waiting around in the cold with us, get yourselves home to the warm," said Mary. Her eyes were glistening and Bronte suspected she wanted them to go before she properly began to cry. Peter put his arm round her.

Breaking free with a "Now don't you start fussing," Mary came over and gave Bronte a quick hug, "You look after him," she whispered affectionately into Bronte's ear.

Bronte and Ryan walked back to the car in silence. Bronte took his hand and gave it a squeeze. "You'll see them again soon," she said.

"I know. The house will just seem rather quiet without them, I guess."

Bronte spent the short journey home doing her best to make Ryan smile. He chatted along, but his usual spark was missing. Pulling up outside their gates, the pair automatically went into Bronte's cottage.

"Have you got time for a quick cuppa before you leave for work?" she said.

"Yeah. My first patient's not until ten."

Bronte made them both tea.

"My family really liked you, you know," Ryan said.

"I really liked them too, they're lovely."

"It made such a difference having you in London. I think I would have gone a little bit crazy in all those clothes shops without you."

"Caitlin seemed to have a good time, didn't she?"

"Yeah, it's funny how she can be so teenagery one minute, and then so excited about going for afternoon tea the next."

"Growing up, eh? Thank goodness we don't have to go through that again!"

The conversation gently flowed, until Ryan reluctantly drained the last of his mug.

"I'd better go. Do you fancy a ride tomorrow morning?"

"Sure, that would be great."

"I'll set it up."

They stood and Ryan gave Bronte a hug and kissed her cheek. His lips lingered for slightly longer than was strictly necessary. She pulled away gently, yet her heartbeat pounded in her chest, betraying her. She mustered a goofy grin to defuse the tension which hung momentarily in the air between them.

"Get going then," she chided, "I'll see you tomorrow."

* * *

Bronte was looking forward to her writers' meeting on Wednesday evening, especially since her car was now fixed and she didn't have to rely on anyone else to drive her. It had been a very productive fortnight. She'd let her characters do what they seemed determined to do, which had led to a rather unexpected result: Pippa and Douglas, her heroine and her hero's brother, had kissed. They hadn't meant to, she hadn't meant them to. It went against everything Pippa thought she'd wanted, and yet it had happened, and it felt right. What would her fellow authors think though? Would they agree, or would they advise her to rewrite her manuscript and put her heroine back with the man she'd originally been destined for, rather than the far less conventional hero she appeared to have chosen for herself. And even if the others thought she was doing the right thing, what would her publishers think when she sent them the manuscript? It was quite a departure from her usual work, but she didn't have time to write anything else, and they'd been chasing her for something for a few weeks now. That wasn't their fault, she admitted: having abandoned her original storyline for the new Pippa and Douglas plot, her promises as to when the book would be ready had become . . . a little elastic. Still, these things couldn't be rushed, and she was proud of what she'd written. It seemed far more honest, and even more romantic than her initial theme, and the latest path of its narrative was now just so much more unusual. She could really imagine Pippa and Douglas having a wonderful future together.

* * *

Once again, she was a little apprehensive about presenting her work and left her reading until the very end of the session. She led into it by explaining what had gone on since she'd last shared the story with them. They listened intently, Bronte's romances were a real guilty pleasure for them, and they especially loved it when she got to the Happy Ever After.

Bronte read her last chapter with her head down, not looking up to gauge her friends' reactions until the very end. When she spoke the final words, she was rewarded with a round of applause. She blushed as almost everyone in the pub turned to find out what was going on.

Camille hugged her. "Congratulations, sweetie, it's fantastic!"

"Are you sure it's romantic enough?"

"It's extremely romantic!"

"Does the brother work as a hero? He's not very dashing is he?"

"He's brilliant! He's real."

"I liked your other heroes, but he's definitely my favourite. He's believable," piped up another voice.

"I'm not sure I'll let my wife read this one," said Norman, "It might give her ideas. She'll never settle for me if she believes there are men like that available."

The praise came from all quarters, bringing with it a swell of relief. They really did like it! The ending worked for them. The comments were universally positive, and seemingly all genuine; the rather unorthodox match up appeared to strike a chord. However, despite the acclaim, Bronte still had doubts.

"But what about my original hero? Would it be better if I changed it back to the heroine falling in love with him?"

"Absolutely not, he wasn't right for her."

"Nowhere near as interesting a character."

"He's rich and handsome and rather strapping don't you think?" said Bronte.

"But would you actually want to spend the rest of your life with him?" Camille asked pointedly.

Bronte paused. "Well . . . no," she answered truthfully. No woman with any gumption would, she thought.

* * *

Camille and Bronte set off the next morning to find a dress for Bronte to wear to the ball.

"I can't believe you've left it so late!" scolded Camille, "You'd better just pray you see something you like because you'll struggle to get anything delivered in time if you have to resort to the internet."

They travelled into London and before they hit the shops, Bronte treated Camille to an early lunch in one of her friend's favourite French bistros as a thank you.

London was much quieter than it had been at the weekend. The great thing about shopping with Camille was that she was an expert. It rarely took as long as you thought it would — she always knew precisely what she was after and exactly where to get it. She took Bronte to Selfridges, eschewed the offer of a personal shopper, and set to work.

Bronte was a little uneasy thanks to the rather over-the-top riding outfit incident, but Camille maintained she'd been right, "It's not my fault you threw yourself off a horse and then only rode with your next-door neighbour in a field down the road. If I'd realised that's what you were shopping for, I would have recommended Primark," she claimed.

"Fair point," mumbled Bronte.

"Everyone really enjoyed your reading last night," Camille said, adding another dress to Bronte's already rather full arms.

"I was so nervous about it."

"Well, it definitely wasn't how any of us expected the story to end." Seeing Bronte's face, she quickly added, "But it was absolutely right!"

"Are you sure?"

"Of course, it felt completely natural that it should happen. The laird was boring, if your heroine had married him she would have just spent the rest of her life holed up in that horrible, draughty castle. His brother might not have been much good at dashing around the countryside on his stallion," she said meaningfully. "But he's kinder and more interesting. He's a much better match for her. That's far more important than what he does for a living or how thick his thighs are."

"I just hope my publishers feel the same way. I'm planning some tweaking tonight and a final read-through tomorrow."

"I'm sure they will. They've just got to give your new hero a chance." Camille waited a moment before adding, "Like you ought to give Ryan a chance."

"I like Ryan, but we're just friends."

"He'd like to be more."

"I don't think so. Well, maybe at first, but neither of us would want to ruin what we've got now," said Bronte, studiously suppressing the memory of Ryan's lingering kiss on her cheek a few days before. "And think of the mess if it didn't work out — we're next-door neighbours!"

"What about if someone else comes along? Someone who sees just how great he is."

"If he liked her, then I'd be pleased for him. Just like I'm pleased for you when someone you like, likes you back. It's what friends do."

"So you're sure you'd be perfectly happy if another woman came along and started a relationship with Ryan."

"Yes," said Bronte, not making eye contact and concentrating very hard on the material of the dress she was holding.

"You're a terrible liar, Bronte. Don't say I didn't warn you. A fantastic guy like that isn't going to stay single for long, trust me."

"Ryan's great, and maybe, if it weren't for Sebastian . . ." she trailed off uncomfortably.

"I knew it!"

"No! It makes no difference, I'm seeing Sebastian. He's the man I'm meant to be with."

"Are you sure about that?"

"Yes, absolutely! You don't create as many heroes as I have without being able to recognise one in real life," she joked.

"OK!" said Camille, holding her hands up in mock surrender, "Why don't you try some of these on? We need to get you looking absolutely amazing for Saturday night. The young lord's date will be the belle of the ball."

"Thanks, Camille," said Bronte, grateful to be putting aside the tricky subject of Ryan, and taking an armful of dresses into the changing room.

* * *

That evening, Bronte returned home tired but happy from another successful riding lesson with Ryan. She and Gwendoline were getting on famously and she was feeling much more confident, although she still definitely preferred walking to trotting! Her earlier conversation with Camille had left her a bit unsure of how to act around Ryan, but luckily dealing with the horse had taken up all her attention and meant she couldn't focus on her neighbour, and whether there was any truth in what Camille had said.

She settled down to edit with a large cup of tea but was interrupted almost immediately by the telephone ringing.

"Hello?"

"Bronte! It's Sebastian. How are you?"

"Hi, I'm good, thanks."

"Marvellous. I'm back on the estate and I've got some friends arriving early for the ball. I thought you might like to come riding with us tomorrow afternoon. I've got a decent mount for you. You do ride, don't you?" he added as an afterthought.

"Er, yes . . . of course, but . . ."

"Splendid! We'll be setting off from the house at two, just for an hour or so. Fancy it?"

"Sure," replied Bronte, summoning up her courage and ignoring her screaming common sense. This was why she was learning to ride, wasn't it? And things were going very well, weren't they? So, carpe diem and all that! "I'll be there."

"See you then!" said Sebastian cheerfully and ended the call.

Off the phone, self-doubt and its close cousin, self-preservation, wormed their nefarious way to the fore of Bronte's mind. Would she embarrass herself terribly the following day? She really wasn't a very competent rider and she didn't want to hold everyone else up as she cautiously plodded along.

No, it would be fine, she answered herself. It was just a little afternoon ride, she'd be able to take it as easy as she needed to. And there were bound to be others there who wanted to take it slowly.

She was really beginning to enjoy riding, and hopefully it would mean she finally had something to talk to Sebastian about. Should she wear her proper riding gear? She imagined Sebastian and his friends would be in full kit; she couldn't envisage Sebastian galloping around the countryside in jeans and an old sweater like Ryan did!

* * *

Bronte pulled up outside Fenworth at half past one. She'd wanted to have plenty of time to get her horse sorted out without keeping everyone else waiting but didn't want to arrive too early in case lunch was still going on.

Preparations were clearly very much underway for the ball. Delivery trucks were parked all around and people were bustling to and fro. There were also plenty of very fancy cars outside the house — Bentleys, Porsches, Range Rovers, even a Maclaren; Bronte's tatty little Mini looked rather out of place amongst them. She'd worn the riding gear Camille had helped her to pick out and hoped she'd made the right decision. Maybe she should have popped a back-up outfit in the car just in case?

She knocked on the doors. There was no reply, but when she pushed, they swung open.

In contrast to her last visit to the house, lights were on, fires were lit, and the whole place seemed far more welcoming.

She stood aside as two men went through the front doors carrying crates of champagne, and tried to ask one of the many people hurrying busily about the entrance hall where Sebastian was, but by the time she'd opened her mouth, they'd moved on, so she quickly gave up on the idea.

The large room with the covered furniture, which she'd seen on the night of the disastrous supper, was full of people. They all seemed to be in their twenties and thirties, so were presumably the friends Sebastian had mentioned rather than guests of his parents'. Not one of them was wearing riding clothes.

Nobody acknowledged Bronte when she entered. A few people glanced up but went immediately back to their conversations when they saw Bronte wasn't someone they knew.

Bronte scanned around and chose the friendliest, most approachable looking woman to speak to, "Um, excuse me, but do you know where Sebastian is?"

"Sebastian?"

"Yes, he lives here . . ."

"Oh! You mean Winky! Has anyone seen Winky?" she brayed.

"I think he went to get changed," a posh voice called over.

"Thanks!" replied Bronte, not quite sure what to do next as all the briefly interrupted conversations resumed about her. She stood there awkwardly, trying to decide whether or not to introduce herself. Thankfully, Sebastian chose that moment to sweep in, sporting full riding gear and looking quite ridiculously rugged and handsome. Bronte instantly cheered up — helped, in no small part by discovering she was in fact dressed appropriately.

"Bronte, you're here!" he proclaimed, taking her in his arms and kissing her exuberantly. She stepped back a little, feeling a bit embarrassed by his rather public display of affection, "Hey, guys, this is Bronte, my girlfriend." A few half-hearted "hellos" were thrown in Bronte's direction, which she didn't really acknowledge as she was still processing the fact that Sebastian had just introduced her to all his 'chums' as his girlfriend. Could she really be termed that? They'd only been out on four dates, none of which had gone particularly well. She felt a little uneasy, even though she knew having a man like Sebastian as her boyfriend was precisely what she'd been hoping for. Their 'relationship' just being announced in front of a load of people she didn't know just seemed to make it feel even more false than she worried it actually was.

Sebastian sat down in a vacant armchair and patted his knee. Bronte reluctantly perched uncomfortably on his thigh, feeling thoroughly silly.

Sebastian draped an arm around her and rattled away to his friends. Eventually, perhaps sensing Bronte's discomfort, the woman she'd spoken to about Sebastian's whereabouts started up a conversation with her, which swiftly slid with awful familiarity into the realms of polo. I really must at least google it, thought Bronte to herself, so that my knowledge of the sport isn't solely based on about 5 minutes of Pretty Woman.

* * *

After what seemed like a lifetime but was probably just an interminable ten minutes, people started to drift away and re-emerge in their riding clothes. Sebastian suggested they go down to the stables and get saddled up.

The group wandered around the outside of the house to the stable block. Everyone else seemed to know exactly where they were going and what to do, and walked confidently over to whichever stall their horse was stabled in. Bronte's feeling of being out of her depth returned tenfold. Sebastian was too busy nattering to his friends and sorting out his own mount to notice she needed help. Standing about like a lemon, she looked desperately around for someone to tell her what she needed to do. Even knowing which horse was supposed to be for her would have been a help. She spotted what she assumed was a stable boy of some kind, and went over to speak to him, "Excuse me, could you help? I'm supposed to be borrowing a horse for the ride, but I'm not sure which is mine."

"Certainly, miss, I expect it'll be Uggle Bug, first stall down there on the right. You'll have no trouble keeping up with the others on him."

A sense of foreboding came over Bronte as she walked slowly over. Peering in, she immediately saw that the horse she'd been given was far bigger than Gwendoline, or even Blossom, come to think of it. Jet black, the sleek, heavily muscled animal looked, as far as she knew, like a thorough-bred racehorse. He tossed his mane haughtily, as if sensing his timidly approaching rider would not be worthy of him. Thankfully, he was already saddled up and set to go, so one hurdle at least was crossed!

His reins were loosely knotted and attached to a hook on the wall. Doing her best to appear confident and in control, Bronte went into the enclosure, undid the knot and led Uggle Bug out into the yard where everyone else was gathering. Most of the other riders were mounted and looking very comfortable. Uggle Bug was so tall that Bronte knew she had no hope of getting up on him without some sort of assistance. She led him slowly over to a low stone wall, all the time trying to maintain her air of poise and assuredness.

Uggle Bug gave her a rather withering look but deigned to stand still long enough for her to hoist herself up onto his back. Once she had her feet in the stirrups and the reins firmly arranged in her hands, the horse's wide back meant she felt surprisingly safe, despite being much higher than she was used to being on Gwendoline.

The other horses began walking out of the stable yard through a narrow gateway. Though a rather milling throng, they had their own hierarchy, and there was certainly a natural order which the horses wanted to go through. Bronte urged Uggle Bug forward, hoping to get near Sebastian's horse so they could ride alongside each other. But Uggle Bug had other ideas. He didn't seem to like the other horses at all and refused to go near any of them. His ears flattened and he bared his teeth, pawing the ground and swishing his tail wildly. She decided to let him hold back, for fear he'd really lose his temper, and did her best to appear nonchalant and like she was in some sort of control of the situation.

Uggle Bug waited until all the others had passed through the gate before following with an air of what Bronte could only describe as arrogance. Bronte needn't have worried about his and her behaviour seeming peculiar to the group: no one was paying either of them any attention anyway.

Just as she thought there was a chance he'd fall in line behind the other horses, he bent his head down suddenly and began chewing on a patch of grass by the side of the track. Bronte slid forward precariously in the saddle, but managed to hold on. By a whisker.

"Come on, boy," she said, making clicking noises with her tongue and pulling on the reins to turn his head. But Uggle Bug was having none of it: he wanted his grass, and he was going to take his own sweet time having it. Bronte watched in despair as everyone else's horses continued along the path ahead and then began to trot, their riders nattering away, and receding into the distance. She considered calling out for help, but she'd have felt even more stupid if someone had to turn back to rescue her. Then, when she thought all hope was lost and she'd have to try to dismount somehow and lead him on foot, Uggle Bug decided he'd had enough of the grass and was prepared to move on. He even began trotting when Bronte bravely squeezed her knees against him. She was thrilled with herself and had to refrain from calling out in excitement to the others, who would no doubt think she was crazy.

But her euphoria was short-lived: without changing his gait, Uggle Bug swerved onto a side track. This time Bronte couldn't have called for help even if she'd wanted to, her whole attention was taken up by the low-hanging branches across the path. She lay as flat as she could against Uggle Bug's neck and frantically tried to figure out what to do, but not before she'd got a couple of nasty scratches on her face.

The horse carried her rapidly along the weaving trail. He seemed quite happy and sure of where he was going, but the way didn't seem at all well-worn, presumably the trees and brambles would have been cut back if it were a popular route.

The woods eventually cleared and the path led to a huge empty field. Bronte sat up straight and pulled on the reins to get Uggle Bug to slow down to a walk, but the delight of seeing the wide open space was clearly too much for him, and he began to canter and then, horror of horrors, actually gallop. There was nothing Bronte could do but hold on for dear life, she doubted there was even any sense in shouting for help — goodness only knew how far away Sebastian and his friends were!

Uggle Bug raced across the entire field, moving so fast his hooves barely seemed to touch the ground, and then leapt over the fence at the far end and landed right in a deep, muddy puddle. Bronte squealed as she got soaked; the sudden cold took her breath away. The horse continued without pause across the next vast field, his snorts coming hard and fast, and over another fence. Bronte had no idea how on earth she was still on his back, her terror must have been lending her strength, but she doubted she could carry on much further, her arms and thighs were trembling now. He'd made it most of the way over the third field, and she was anticipating another fence jump when the horse abruptly stopped and Bronte almost went flying straight over his head.

Uggle Bug looked around, as if catching his breath and getting his bearings. Bronte kept her grip on the reins tight, anxiously wondering what on earth he was going to do next. He began to walk solemnly towards a large gap in a hedge. He went through it and continued down a gentle slope until they reached a gravel track. Thank goodness they were out of those fields, was all Bronte kept thinking to herself, she couldn't have faced another jump. She desperately wanted to get off but couldn't see anything she could use to get down.

Her face was sore from the scratches and covered in mud, but she didn't dare take a hand off the reins to wipe it.

Uggle Bug walked calmly down the path, stopping every now and again to have a sniff at something or munch on some grass. Bronte had completely given up trying to exert any sort of control over the animal. She wished she'd brought her mobile with her, but she'd left it in the car, not thinking she'd need it.

Bronte's arms and legs were now burning from holding on so tightly. She kept glancing about, as much as she dared to without unbalancing herself. She didn't recognise any of the countryside around her, which was hardly surprising as she hadn't even driven around this area very much before, let alone gone riding here.

They reached the top of a small hill and Bronte's heart lifted with relief and she laughed out loud. She could see Sebastian's house in the distance! She sat up as straight as she could and lifted herself up in the saddle in an attempt to work out how to get back there. Should she somehow get off Uggle Bug and lead him? It looked quite far, and what if he ran off? She'd never get him back, and she didn't think Sebastian would be too impressed if she lost one of his horses. Judging by how much he loved riding, it would lead to her being well and truly dumped!

Uggle Bug was now definitely heading in the direction of home, and Bronte figured all she could do was put her trust in him. If he started to veer completely off course she'd just have to jump off, she decided, gulping at the thought.

As it happened, there was no need for her to worry: Uggle Bug was tired and looking forward to getting back to his nice warm stable. He seemed to even know how long they were supposed to be out for; they approached the stable blocks again almost at the exact moment the other riders returned. Uggle Bug seemed to have got over his hatred of the rest of his kind, and fell into step at the head of the gang.

Sebastian rode up beside her. "Bronte! There you are! Did you have a good little jaunt? I don't think I saw you once! It looks like you had fun anyway!" he remarked, looking at her clothes.

Bronte looked down and, with horror, took in the state of her attire: she was splattered from head to toe with mud and goodness only knows what else. She'd been so intent on holding on and making it back in one piece, she hadn't considered the mess she must be in. He must think she was a total disaster!

"Yeah, great fun," she answered as breezily as possible.

"I'm surprised you went out on old Uggle Bug, temperamental blighter — he's got a bit of a mind of his own! Must've known who was boss this time though, eh?"

"I guess so," replied Bronte through gritted teeth. She was furious with Sebastian: if he'd been paying her any sort of consideration at all she wouldn't be on this crazy horse and she wouldn't have ended up in this state! She couldn't help but feel Ryan would never have put her in such a situation, he was always so careful and considerate, a complete contrast to Sebastian's careless attitude.

Sebastian rode off to join some of his friends.

She spotted the stable boy who'd sent her to Uggle Bug, "Excuse me!" she called to him, "Would you give me a hand down please?"

She received a few disparaging looks from those around her, but she no longer cared. She was frozen, dirty, wet and aching and wanted to be off the horse immediately.

Sensing how annoyed she was, the stable boy came straight over. He held Uggle Bug steady and helped her off, then led the horse to his stall.

Bronte's legs almost gave out when she reached the ground. She'd never spent that long on a horse before. She discreetly shook them to try to get some feeling to return.

Soon everyone was relieved of their rides and began traipsing back to the house, chatting away, the other women still looking immaculate. Bronte shuffled soggily along behind them.

Entering the grand house, she stopped: she couldn't go and sit down in one of those antique chairs when she was so filthy! She'd ruin it! Could you even get mud out of upholstery that old? She doubted it. Lingering until she spotted Sebastian, she went over to him. "I think I'd better get back home."

"Oh! I hoped you'd stay. We're all going to have dinner, it'll be fun," he said, moving towards her, but thinking better of it when he saw quite how filthy she was.

"Sorry, I didn't bring a change of clothes."

"Perhaps someone can lend you something," Sebastian said, looking around as if he expected a rail of clothes in Bronte's size to appear beside them.

"Thanks, but I'd rather go home," Bronte said firmly, "I'll see you tomorrow evening."

"Alright, if you're sure," said Sebastian, giving her a kiss, "Until then."

Bronte hurried to her little car and turned the heating up high. She drove back, once again shivering all the way and cursing Sebastian, the stable boy and Uggle Bug in equal measure.

* * *

Pulling up in front of her cottage, she climbed gingerly out of the Mini and turned to examine the muck-covered front seat. Good job she wasn't planning on going anywhere else today!

The sound of an engine drew her attention; oh for goodness sake, did Ryan really have to choose this time to get home from work?

"Hey," he called out pleasantly, opening his car door, "How's my favourite author doing?"

"Well, I don't know how Danielle Steel is, but I'm fine."

He laughed, "Want to join me for a cuppa?"

"Um . . . sure. Let's have it in my house though, I need to change."

Ryan had by now made his way around to their garden gates and could properly see her and the state of her outfit, for the first time.

"You alright?" he asked, the barely suppressed urge to laugh clear on his face.

"Yes, of course." Bronte opted to pass off the situation with breezy aloofness.

"It's just you're covered in mud and wearing your riding gear."

"Sebastian invited me to go riding with him and some of his friends."

"And you ended up like that?" he chortled.

"Well, it's quite muddy out there."

"You don't say?" he replied, grinning.

Bronte realised there was no getting out of explaining what had really happened.

"My horse decided it didn't think much of the other horses or the route they were taking, so took me on a bit of a detour. But on the plus side, I've tried galloping and jumping five-bar gates."

"What!?" Ryan exclaimed, his cheerful mood suddenly replaced with indignation, "Why on earth didn't he look after you properly? You could have been seriously hurt!"

"You sound like my father," muttered Bronte. Ryan ignored this, so she continued, "I don't think he realised I needed looking after. I didn't tell him I was a beginner."

"Whyever not?"

"I was embarrassed," she admitted. "Everyone he knows has been riding forever, and I didn't want to be the odd one out or make him feel he had to spend all the afternoon watching me and worrying that I couldn't manage."

"But clearly you couldn't manage!"

"Yes, I see that now," answered Bronte, hotly, "But I'm fine. There's no need to have a go at me, I'm completely aware of how stupid I was, thank you, I don't require you to tell me as well."

"Sorry," said Ryan, and gave her a hug, "I'm just going over worst-case scenarios in my head and stressing about the danger you were in, but it seems like you're OK, if a bit frozen. Why don't you go and get warmed up and I'll make you a genuine Irish coffee? That'll sort you out."

"Thanks for worrying about me. An Irish coffee would be lovely."

Bronte went upstairs, very grateful to be home and to have such a good friend.

* * *

Ryan didn't stay long, and after he'd left, Bronte went back to her bedroom to have another look at her outfit for the ball. She wanted something to rekindle her fondness for Sebastian. Notwithstanding what she'd said to Ryan, he was definitely still in her bad books.

She was thrilled with the dress Camille had helped her pick out: she'd never owned anything quite so glamorous before, and it felt bizarrely grown-up. She hung it on her bedroom door and took a step back to admire it again. It really was beautiful.

She'd also splashed out on shoes and a clutch bag. The shoes were about as high as she could possibly manage to both walk and dance in. She anticipated rather sore feet by the end of the night, but it would be worth it. She was just glad her ankle appeared to be fine now. It had held up today without mishap.

It was ending up being a very expensive occasion, but Bronte reasoned this might be her only opportunity to go to a ball, so she may as well make the most of it and do things properly. Then again, if things continued going well with Sebastian, there could be plenty more events like this to look forward to in the future, so she'd better get used to them!

However, she told herself firmly, Cinders wouldn't be going to any ball if she didn't get her manuscript sent off.

She made herself a huge mug of tea and unplugged the phone before taking her laptop back up to her bedroom and climbing into bed for what had become her final read-through ritual. Blocking everything else from her mind, she focussed absolutely on her story and the characters unfolding before her.

She stopped for some supper but apart from that worked right through until she was finished, by which time it was almost one in the morning. Her eyes were a little sore from staring at the computer screen for so long, and she was pretty tired, but above all there was a sense of accomplishment. The book was done, and she was proud of it. Camille was right: this story did feel more real and, in a way, more romantic because of the changes. This romance was the beginning of a lifetime love. The heroine and her rather unorthodox hero seemed made for each other. Sending the email with the Word file of her book attached, Bronte just hoped that her editor agreed.

CHAPTER ELEVEN

Turning off her hairdryer the following evening, Bronte checked the clock on the bedside table. Camille would be arriving soon. Bronte was in her dress, and her make-up was done; all that was left was for her friend to help with her hair. Looking out of the bedroom window, she saw Camille's car was parked outside the cottages, her hairdryer must have drowned out the sound of her arrival.

She called out and went downstairs, but there was no reply. Where was Camille? Bronte opened the front door wondering if she was waiting outside, but it wasn't locked, so presumably her friend would have just come in. Then she heard voices carrying through the wall connecting her home to Ryan's; two voices, one male and one female.

Slightly puzzled, Bronte pulled on a pair of trainers and went out to say hi and see how close Ryan was to being ready.

Her knock took a long time to be answered. Finally the door opened, and there stood Camille. She was dressed in a full-length black halter-necked gown which brought out the deep green of her huge eyes. Her long, wavy hair was piled up on top of her head, and she looked amazing. Everything about her screamed class and perfection. Mirroring the appraisal, Camille smiled at Bronte, until her gaze reached

Bronte's feet, "Not sure about the choice of footwear, darling," she said with a laugh.

"Don't worry, I'm going to change them."

"Hiya, Bronte," Ryan called out from the kitchen, "Would you like a drink? I was just pouring Camille and I a glass of wine."

He came into the doorway, bottle in his hand. He was wearing his tuxedo trousers, but his shirt was open and loose. He must have been disturbed by Camille while he was getting dressing, she thought uncertainly. Bronte's heart rate began to quicken at the sight of him. She had to admit he was absolutely gorgeous. Pulling herself away from the fantasies that were swiftly forming in her mind, she said rather primly, "Why don't you go and finish getting yourself dressed and I'll pour the wine?"

"Actually, I was rather enjoying the scenery," flirted Camille.

Ryan handed Bronte the bottle, being in such close contact with his naked chest meant she very nearly dropped it. He went upstairs, "Sorry, Camille," he said, giving her a wink.

Camille watched Ryan until he disappeared from view, while a rather uncomfortable Bronte studiously made sure not to.

"Spoilsport," Camille whispered.

"You're incorrigible."

"I know, but you've got to confess, that's one fantastic body."

Bronte judged it best not to reply and concentrated on pouring out the drinks.

"Hadn't we better go to my house if you're still happy to sort out my hair?"

"We could do it here," said Camille.

"All my stuff is next door," Bronte replied, "And anyway, I don't really want you doing my hair in front of Ryan."

"Why not? He's only a friend, isn't he?" said Camille.

"I'd just rather do it over there."

"OK," shrugged Camille. "Ryan," she called up the stairs, "we're just going next door to sort out Bronte's hair, we'll be back soon."

"Sure!" came the reply, "See you in a bit."

They walked round to Bronte's cottage.

"Why didn't you come to my house straight away?" probed Bronte.

"I knocked, but you didn't answer, and then Ryan spotted me and invited me in."

That all sounded pretty reasonable, but Bronte couldn't shake the feeling that there was more to it: Camille had appeared very comfortable with Ryan and had seemed rather reluctant to leave. And Camille knew that Bronte usually left her door unlocked, wouldn't it have been more natural for Camille to go to her friend's first?

Camille had mentioned before that she found Ryan attractive, and she'd obviously enjoyed the view of him with his shirt undone. Was her friend planning on making a move on Ryan tonight? The thought left her decidedly unhappy. She pushed it very firmly to the back of her mind so she could focus on what Camille was suggesting for her hair and keep her face neutral.

"Fabulous!" Camille declared when she was finished putting Bronte's hair up in a chic 1920s style side bun, "Sebastian won't be able to concentrate on anything but you tonight, you're stunning."

But Bronte wasn't thinking about Sebastian as she studied herself in her mirror. She couldn't help but be far more interested in how Ryan would react. Her dress wasn't quite as sexy as Camille's backless number, but she loved it: pale blue and with a full skirt, it was strapless and reached halfway down her calves. She'd chosen it because it was just like something Grace Kelly might have worn.

She smiled. "Thanks for your help, Camille."

"No problem. Shall we get back next door and have that glass of wine? It won't be long before the taxi's here to pick us up."

"OK," replied Bronte, trying to suppress her discomfort at how eager her friend was to get back to Ryan.

The man in question was now fully dressed and doing up his bow tie.

Camille slunk over to him, "Let me help with that," she purred.

Bronte glanced away, embarrassed. It certainly appeared that Camille had made up her mind to make a play for Ryan. And he appeared very happy to go along with whatever she had planned.

"You look great," Ryan said to Bronte — a little absent-mindedly, she felt.

"Thanks," replied Bronte, but wasn't sure Ryan heard her, as Camille chose that exact moment to ask whether he could check at the back of her dress, to make sure it was done up properly.

"Seems fine to me," said Ryan, "Right, have you ladies both got everything you need?"

"I think so," said Bronte.

"I'm all set," said Camille, "Would you be able to take a photo of Ryan and me please, Bronte?" she asked, handing Bronte her phone, "I think we look pretty good together, don't you, Ryan?"

She snaked her arm around him. He didn't reply, but he certainly wasn't fighting her off. Bronte quickly took the photograph and was very grateful to hear the beep of the taxi horn outside.

Camille was fast off the mark. "I'll take the back seat with you, Ryan. Bronte, you go in the front with the driver, that way you'll be able to help him with directions if he's not sure where to go."

Of course he'll know where Fenworth is, thought Bronte testily as she got into the front passenger seat, trying to block out Camille's throaty laughs coming from the back.

* * *

The whole of the driveway was lined with flaming torches. "Wow! It looks gorgeous," said Camille, gazing open-mouthed out of the taxi window.

Bronte felt butterflies fluttering around in her stomach as they came to a halt outside the house. Light and music poured from the stately home, and excited chatter filled the evening air.

"I'll be picking you all up at one, I think," said the driver.

"I won't need a cab later, thanks," Bronte replied. "I'll spend the night here," she said to Ryan and Camille. Ryan's face gave nothing away, but Camille raised an eyebrow and said, "OK then, it'll just be the two of us being picked up."

Ryan offered Camille his arm as she got out of the car, and they walked to the house together, with Bronte traipsing after them, feeling like a bit of a third wheel. She hoped she could find Sebastian quickly so she'd have someone to partner with.

Bronte handed the invitations to the doorman, who directed them inside to where Sebastian's parents were waiting to greet the guests.

Ensuring she had a friendly smile on her face, Bronte said, "Good evening, Lord Fairfax, Lady Fairfax."

"Good evening," replied Sebastian's mother, clearly unable to place her. His father just gave her a blank stare.

"It's Bronte, I had supper with you a couple of weeks ago."

"Oh right, well I do hope you enjoy your evening." She turned to address her husband, "Come darling, Horatio's arrived." The pair brushed past them without a second glance as they went to meet this new and far more interesting arrival.

Well, that's put me in my place, thought Bronte. If she and Sebastian were going to work as a couple, she'd really have to think of a way to make his mother and father like her. But now wasn't the time to worry about that. She was determined to make the most of the amazing evening and wasn't going to let their rudeness spoil it for her.

"Golly, she's a bit frosty, isn't she? And what's up with him?" whispered Camille conspiratorially.

"They're probably just really busy," said Bronte, trying her best not to feel humiliated. "They are the hosts after all, and this ball's a big deal to them."

"Come on," said Ryan, "I spy drinks, let's get some and have a look around."

They helped themselves to glasses of champagne from a table set up in the drawing room. Bronte spotted a couple of people she recognised from the previous day's riding, but they'd moved away before she had a chance to go over and say hi.

The trio were having a nose in the ballroom and watching the musicians set up when Bronte was spun around and found herself face to face with Sebastian.

"Ah, the belle of the ball!" he kissed her on the lips, "Are you having a good time?"

"Yes, thanks, it's wonderful," replied Bronte, but feared she'd already lost his attention, as he was waving to someone he recognised out in the hallway before she finished her sentence.

A gong was struck and supper was announced. Ryan took Camille's arm to walk her into the dining room. Bronte glanced about for Sebastian, but he'd disappeared again. She eventually gave up and walked in by herself.

The dining room was enormous, which was lucky as it needed to accommodate an awful lot of tables and chairs. Bronte knew more people were due to arrive after the meal, but already there were about sixty guests. One long table ran across the far end of the room, and it was here Bronte found her name by a place setting. Smaller round tables, each seating between six and ten people and beautifully laid with a gold candelabrum as their centrepiece, were set out around the rest of the room. Ryan and Camille had ended up on the same distant table and looked like they were enjoying themselves.

Bronte was sandwiched between two elderly gentlemen, presumably friends of Lord Fairfax. She introduced herself, and made several attempts at polite conversation, but her repartee only had the effect of diverting their attention from their wine to her cleavage.

Sebastian was one of the last to come into the room and took his place at the foot of Bronte's table.

Bronte kept glancing over rather enviously at Camille and Ryan, feeling a bit put out that they seemed to be having a much better time than she was. They were laughing and smiling. She noticed Ryan was being very attentive, making sure Camille's wine glass remained full and that she had everything she needed.

Sebastian caught her eye and raised his glass to her a couple of times, but he was busy being the young heir to the estate, holding court to everyone at his end of the table about polo or horses, she guessed. She considered getting up and going to talk to him, but was certain that wasn't 'the done thing' at this sort of event and didn't want to show him up. She'd see plenty of him after dinner.

The food was delicious, if a little in the nursery-vein which Bronte was rapidly learning Sebastian and his family favoured. She could see that Lord Fairfax wasn't overly impressed with the beef Wellington by his more than usually sour face and the way he pushed his food around his plate after tasting it. She was also sure she'd lip-read Lady Fairfax say to him, "I'll warm you up something else later, dear."

Bronte took the opportunity to take in the other guests and the room itself. There were only about eight people under fifty apart from her, Sebastian, Ryan and Camille. She recognised most of them from the day before. The other diners seemed to be mainly old friends of Sebastian's parents: well-heeled, aristocratic and a bit dull. Nobody else appeared as awestruck as she was at the grandeur of their surroundings. Sebastian was obviously used to this sort of thing, and Ryan and Camille were too interested in each other to pay attention to what was around them, she thought a little bitterly — but then sternly berated herself: she was being selfish and ridiculous. Of course she wanted them both to be happy, and if they happened to find that happiness together, how wonderful!

And Ryan could still be her friend as well as Camille's lover; there was no reason why anything had to change on that score. Plus, if things worked out with Sebastian, she'd naturally have less time to spend with Ryan. She'd only known him a couple of months, and she'd managed perfectly well without him before he'd moved into the cottage next door.

Maybe Sebastian would want her to come and live in Fenworth with him? But then she'd be living with his awful parents as well, and she really wasn't sure she could cope with that! He tended to spend most of his time in London, but presumably much of that would also be alongside Lord and Lady Fairfax. Besides which, she had absolutely no desire to up sticks back to London. Yet she couldn't imagine Sebastian agreeing to live in her tiny home with his arch enemy Mr Darcy! She supposed, if they did move in together, she'd have to find a new home for her cat. The thought unexpectantly made her well up. She knew he was an awkward, cantankerous creature, but he'd kept her company since she'd been at her cottage, and she couldn't imagine being without him.

She'd chosen him from the rescue centre because she'd felt so sorry for him. He'd had to be kept all by himself because he didn't get on with any of the other animals. He was skinny and his coat was dull. He'd been huddled in the furthest corner of his pen, looking sad and dejected; the sight of him just broke Bronte's heart. The staff said they weren't sure of his history, but he'd clearly been badly treated in the past. How could she reject him now?

She wiped her tears away, hoping no one had noticed. She was being silly. What she was considering would be way, way in the future, if it happened at all. There was absolutely no need to worry about it now.

Taking a deep gulp of wine, she pulled herself together. She was so lucky to be here, in this fabulous place, and as the date of the lord of the manor's son! She'd been to plenty of amazing country houses as research for her books, but walking through the empty halls was very different from actually being at a ball in one!

When dinner was over, the men retired to a smoking room and the women were all ushered into another chamber and served coffee. Bronte was sorry to once again miss the chance of spending some time with Sebastian, who was one of the first up from the dining table, but it was good to be able to catch up with Camille.

"You and Ryan seem to be having a great time," said Bronte, fishing for information as subtly as she could.

"Yes," confirmed her friend. "It's fantastic here! I mean, just look at this place!" Camille exclaimed.

"Ryan seemed to be keeping you entertained over dinner."

"He's excellent company, so funny. And charming too. I didn't realise before."

"Neither did I," said Bronte quietly.

* * *

It wasn't long before the rest of the guests began to arrive. Car after car pulled up on the gravel forecourt, depositing glamorous guests, anxious to get in quickly from the cold night air.

Finally, dancing was announced and everyone moved into the ballroom where the musicians had begun playing a Viennese waltz. Bronte thought there must easily be over two hundred people there now.

Ryan found Bronte and Camille. He admitted to having had a bit of a coughing fit when he took his first puff of cigar. "Sebastian seemed to find it very amusing," he added.

"I'm sure he didn't," said Bronte weakly, feeling she ought to come to her boyfriend's defence, but suspecting that he probably had found the incident rather comical. "He must have been laughing at something else."

Ryan didn't look convinced but brushed it off, "I suppose it was pretty funny."

The three friends watched as the first couples took to the dance floor; they were all very competent. Scarily competent.

Bronte was busy scanning the room for Sebastian, but it seemed he was still enjoying his cigars and 'boy talk.' She turned to speak to her friends and noticed Ryan had his arm around Camille's waist. She looked away quickly.

"Shall we dance?" she heard Ryan ask Camille.

"I'd love to," she said. "Will you be OK?" she checked with Bronte.

"Of course," Bronte replied, overly brightly, "Sebastian will be here in a second."

"If you're sure," called her friend over her shoulder as she was twirled, giggling into the fray.

Bronte watched the waltzers, enjoying the music and the whole experience, but after a while she began to feel a bit awkward. Every other woman under seventy had a partner, and even some of the ancient matrons were moving slowly around the dance floor with their husbands. She was sure it was the duty of the master of the house to ensure all young ladies found a dance partner, but there was no sign of Sebastian's father either. She wasn't surprised there: the port would need careful chaperoning she suspected.

She 'took a turn about the room', hoping that keeping moving would prevent her from looking like such a lemon. She knew she was probably being paranoid, but she could swear some of the other guests were glancing at her pityingly.

She was ready to leave the ballroom and launch a proper search for Sebastian when she felt a gentle tap on her shoulder. She expected it to be her date, and was surprised to discover it was, in fact, Ryan.

"Hey you, having fun?" he asked.

"Yeah, it's wonderful here. Like something out of a fairy tale."

"Just because something's like a fairy tale, doesn't mean that it translates all that well into real life."

Seeing that Bronte looked a bit uncomfortable, Ryan changed the subject, "Camille's just gone to the bathroom."

"Oh, OK."

"Would you like to dance with me?" he asked softly.

Bronte really did want to dance. She'd spent years writing about grand parties and high-society balls, and here she was actually experiencing one, but without the most important part, it seemed: the handsome hero. She knew she should probably wait for Sebastian, but at that moment there was nobody in the world she would rather dance with than Ryan, and before she could stop herself she answered, "Yes, please." Wordlessly, he grasped her hand and led her onto the dance floor.

His arms felt strong and confident as he drew her into them.

"I didn't know you could dance," Bronte whispered to him.

"I guess there's a lot you still don't know about me," he answered, twirling her around expertly, then pulling her close again. She looked up and their eyes met. How had she never noticed how intensely green his eyes were before.

"Bronte . . ." he began with a sigh.

"Yes?"

Ryan went to continue but was interrupted by a cough.

"You don't mind if I steal my date back, do you?" asked Sebastian with a thin smile.

"Of course," replied Ryan coldly, "Bronte, it looks like this dance is already taken."

He let go of her and walked off to join Camille, who'd just come back into the room.

Sebastian took hold of Bronte. She stepped away slightly: she didn't like the way Sebastian had treated Ryan, and she would have preferred to have been asked to dance by Sebastian, not demanded from Ryan like she was his property.

"Are you alright?" Sebastian asked.

"Fine, you were just holding me a little tightly," she said, avoiding a confrontation, once again not wanting to spoil the evening with Sebastian by starting an argument.

To her disappointment, Sebastian was nowhere near as competent a dancer as Ryan, due, at least in part, to the amount of alcohol he'd consumed. He definitely wasn't very coordinated, and Bronte spent most of their foxtrot defending her feet from attack.

It didn't help that Sebastian kept getting distracted by his many friends. Bronte felt she was playing the part of the girlfriend, but not getting the attention she'd expect from the role.

"It's hot in here!" said Sebastian, giving Bronte a last spin at the end of a particularly vigorous dance. "Shall we go outside for a bit to cool down?"

"Sure, just let me get my coat," said Bronte, grateful for the chance of a break.

* * *

The night air was cold, invigoratingly so after the stuffy heat of the ballroom. Bronte wrapped her coat tighter about her. Her outfit of course looked vastly better without it, but she was grateful for its warmth.

Going round the side of the building, they reached a large enclosed patio lit by the full moon and the myriad of radiant windows. A low wrought-iron fence surrounded the terrace and steps led down to a lawn below. In the distance, Bronte could just make out the tennis court and a small woodland, beyond which she knew lay the ruins of the old estate church. It would make a beautiful place to be married.

Adrift in her thoughts, Bronte was taken a little by surprise when Sebastian enveloped her in his arms. He let out an appreciative growl as their lips met, which put Bronte off a bit. She instinctively moved away, but he brought her back to him. She tried to focus on what was going on, to lose herself in the kiss . . . but couldn't. All she could think about was Ryan and what he was doing. Were he and Camille also hidden away in some similarly dark spot?

The thought made her insides feel like they were twisting up.

She had Sebastian's complete attention for the first time this evening, and the relationship definitely seemed to be moving forward physically. This was what she wanted, wasn't it? Yet she found she couldn't have been less interested. She wanted to be in love with him — this was her textbook hero! She wanted to be throwing herself into his arms, overcome with passion. But now that it finally came down to it, she felt practically nothing.

What was she actually doing here with this man? He wasn't the one for her — if she were honest with herself, she'd known that for a long time, she'd not wanted to admit it or give up the hope that somehow the storybook fairytale ending would come about. He may have seemed perfect and 'the one' on paper, but in reality, they simply didn't work. They had absolutely nothing in common, they couldn't even manage a decent conversation. His family were just plain rude, and, while he was certainly good-looking, she realised the initial attraction she'd felt for him had evaporated over time, as she got to know the real him. Exactly the opposite of what had happened as she got to know the real Ryan.

Sebastian's huge frame seemed to dwarf her, and she longed for Ryan's more compact body, which she fitted so easily next to whenever they hugged. Sebastian's just felt uncomfortable: too big and too firm.

With her back to the house, she didn't notice Ryan also coming out for a breath of fresh air. Walking around the corner, he saw Bronte and Sebastian together. He stopped for a moment, then swiftly turned and hurried inside.

"Shall we go up to my room?" Sebastian muttered into Bronte's ear as he stroked her neck.

She panicked: she couldn't sleep with him, not when she'd be thinking about Ryan and wishing she were with him the entire time.

"I'm sorry," she said, pulling away.

Sebastian looked confused, "But we . . ." he started.

"I know, and I'm so sorry. I thought it was what I wanted, but I was wrong."

"It's the Irish guy, isn't it? Your neighbour."

"Yes," admitted Bronte softly.

"He's a dentist!"

"Yep."

"What on earth does he have that I don't?"

"He's right for me," Bronte said, realising it was the truth as she said it.

"He's your soulmate?" said Sebastian sarcastically.

"I don't know. I'm not actually sure I believe in soulmates. But I do know that I can't continue anything with you. I'm really sorry, but I've got to go."

Bronte went to leave, but Sebastian grabbed her arm. "I'm heir to all this, and you're turning me down for a nobody! Just goes to show Mummy and Daddy were right; you're nowhere near good enough for me. I never should have tried slumming it," he sneered vindictively.

"I'm going, Sebastian," said Bronte firmly, removing his hand, "Goodbye."

A braying laugh heralded the arrival of another couple onto the terrace, and she was spared further recriminations.

Bronte felt like racing back inside and throwing herself on Ryan, but she allowed good sense to prevail. She forced herself to take her time walking back around the house, planning what she was going to say. She thought she'd ask to speak to him alone, tell him she'd finished things with Sebastian and ask, as casually as she could manage, if he'd like to go on a date with her. She'd play it cool, she didn't want to risk scaring him off.

She went into the house and worked her way through the crowds of people back into the ballroom. She didn't see Ryan at first and was about to turn and look for him elsewhere when she spotted him in a corner, his arms around Camille, who was whispering in his ear and rubbing his back.

In her excitement at her epiphany, she'd forgotten how close Ryan and her friend were becoming. Now she'd finally discovered that Ryan meant to her, it seemed she was too late.

Devastated, Bronte rushed out of the room. She felt queasy and could feel herself welling up. She had to get away as quickly as possible. Oh, how could she have been such an idiot? If she hadn't wasted so much time on Sebastian, if she'd just realised how fantastic the man next door was . . . She couldn't be angry with them. Ryan had asked her out and she'd turned him down. Camille had tried to tell her how great Ryan was and had advised her to choose him over Sebastian. Bronte had even been the one who'd suggested Camille go after Ryan!

She used her mobile to call the cab company and hid in the bathroom until the driver called to say he was waiting outside. She texted Camille, so her friends wouldn't worry about her:

Going home, got a bit of a headache. Have fun!

At the thought of the 'fun' she knew her two friends were having, her despair painfully deepened and she began to silently weep.

CHAPTER TWELVE

There was good news on Monday morning. When Bronte checked her emails, she discovered a reply from her editor, who'd read the manuscript and loved it.

"It's perfect," she'd concluded.

Contradictorily, this served to make Bronte feel even more wretched: it was another acknowledgement of what really made a relationship. Why was it that one of her characters could see what was right in front of her and recognise a good man when she saw one, yet she, their creator, had been completely incapable of doing the same until it was too late?

She got up and pulled open the sitting-room curtains, looking out hopefully for Ryan's car but knowing it wouldn't be there. It had been gone by the time she rose on Sunday and she hadn't seen it since. Neither had she seen or heard from him. Or Camille. His empty parking space seemed to taunt her, a nagging reminder of just how stupid she'd been.

Since he'd moved in, Bronte hadn't gone so long without chatting to Ryan. Her own home, as well as his, felt empty without him next door. She wondered when he'd be back. Presumably he couldn't stay away forever, he had to go to work and would need clean clothes. Was he planning to move in with Camille? Surely that was a bit quick, but maybe he'd been carrying a torch for her friend for a while, and Bronte just hadn't noticed. She'd been too busy focussing on Sebastian — she was such a fool!

Miserably, she showered and dressed in a baggy t-shirt and tracksuit bottoms. She didn't bother with any make-up, what was the point? The only person she cared about looking nice for was Ryan, and he wasn't there.

She went downstairs and wandered around aimlessly, tidying up a little, looking out of the window frequently, just in case. She was at a bit of a loss what to do. Usually after she submitted a manuscript, she gave herself a little time off to celebrate. She might go shopping and treat herself, perhaps she and Camille would go out for a nice lunch or a spa day. But she couldn't bear the thought of speaking to her friend. She knew it wasn't Camille's fault that she'd got together with Ryan. She'd checked with Bronte often enough that she'd be happy for Ryan to date other people. And knowing Camille, if Bronte had said she'd liked Ryan, she would have stepped aside. No, Bronte had no one to blame for her pain but herself, and she needed to find a way to cope with it before she saw Camille and Ryan together as a couple. They'd be so blissful, in the first flush of a new relationship; she mustn't spoil that for them by appearing anything less than thrilled. Neither of them must ever know or suspect her true feelings.

She'd allow herself a couple of days to feel sorry for herself and then that was it: she'd call Camille, claim illness since the ball and act surprised when she was told about her and Ryan, and then wish them both all the luck in the world — they deserved to be happy with each other.

Bronte dragged her duvet downstairs onto the sofa. She got a box of tissues ready and a pile of her favourite old movies, putting Breakfast at Tiffany's firmly to one side. She didn't want anything that reminded her of Ryan and the great times they'd spent together. She'd begin with To Catch a Thief and plenty of ice cream and chocolate for comfort. She resolved that by the time she'd worked her way through them all, she'd be ready to face Ryan and Camille.

Mr Darcy slunk up and put his paw gently on her knee. He purred softly, then climbed up and put his face next to hers. Bronte stiffened, expecting a swipe, but it didn't come. Instead, the cat settled down with her on the sofa. Bronte gingerly put a hand on him and tickled his head; he purred louder and tucked himself in close, then fell asleep.

* * *

Bronte woke with a jolt. She was still on the sofa with an empty tub of Ben and Jerry's on the floor. It was dark both inside and out. Checking the clock, she saw it was just after seven p.m. She'd had such an interrupted sleep the night before, she must have dropped off in the middle of Gone with the Wind. The menu screen was still up on the television with the iconic theme music playing. The last thing she remembered was Rhett Butler turning up to discover Scarlett O'Hara had got married a second time.

Coming to a little more, she rubbed her eyes and realised someone was knocking on her front door.

"Hang on," she murmured, easing herself up stiffly.

She turned on the light in the hallway and opened the door. It was Ryan.

"Hey," he said softly.

"Hey yourself."

"Um . . . Are you alright? You look terrible."

"Thanks."

"I didn't mean it like that."

"I'm fine, you just caught me napping. I'm having a lazy day."

"Right . . ." Ryan looked slightly nervous, but then seemed to steel himself, "Grab your coat and shoes."

"Where are we—" began Bronte, but she was interrupted by a loud whinny.

"What was that?" she asked in astonishment. Ryan stepped aside. Waiting patiently by the cottages' gates were two horses she immediately recognised as Gwendoline and

Horace. They were hitched to a two-seater open-topped carriage.

"Wow," gasped Bronte.

"I'm just glad it isn't raining. That would have completely messed this up."

Before Bronte could ask any more questions, Ryan reminded her, "Coat and shoes . . ."

Shaking her head in disbelief, she did as she was asked. She locked the front door and approached the carriage. Ryan was waiting to open the little half door, and proffering his hand, helped her up with a solemn, "Allow me." Comfortable on the soft, red seat she waited, breath condensing in the night air, as he climbed in himself and arranged a heavy woollen blanket over their legs. Without a word, he took up the reins and, giving them a sharp snap, started the horses walking.

They didn't speak. Though the November evening was cold, it was beautiful: crisp, fresh and clear. The moon was still full and its subtle radiance flooded the landscape. The bumps and dips of the carriage's passage didn't disturb Bronte, she was lost in thought. Just what was going on? She almost thought she was dreaming; perhaps she was still fast asleep on her sofa. Surely this sort of thing didn't happen in real life?

Trundling softly down the country lanes in the mellow golden pool of light thrown by the carriage lamps, the only sounds that broke the silence were those of the buggy and horses, and the occasional hoot of an owl.

Time slipped hazily by until they slowed to a halt by the edge of a lake. Ryan climbed down and tethered the horses to a tree before helping Bronte out.

"Ryan—" she began, but he put his finger gently on her lips.

"Not yet," he said quietly.

They walked a short distance along the shoreline to where a small table and two chairs were set up. The table was elegantly laid with a crisp white tablecloth, two ornate silver candlesticks and crystal champagne flutes.

Ryan pulled out a chair for a rather confused Bronte to sit on. He carefully lit the candles, then went down to the lake's edge where he picked up a bottle he'd been chilling in the icy water. When he brought it over to the table into the small pool of light, Bronte saw it was champagne. He opened it expertly and poured them both a glass before sitting down in the chair opposite Bronte. He raised his glass to her and took a deep, appreciative glug and sat back.

"Ryan, this is amazing, but what's it all in aid of?" said Bronte, not able to wait any longer for him to explain himself.

He took a moment before answering, "This is me showing you something. I guess it's rather a last-ditch effort."

"What are you trying to show me?" asked Bronte gently.

Ryan fell into silence again, staring out across the moonlit lake. He ran his hands through his hair, and resolve found, turned back to meet her eyes, "I want to show you that I'm more than just a slightly crazy-haired Irish dentist living in his aunt's house. I can be romantic. I can do the grand gesture. I just haven't been brave enough to . . . until now."

"But—"

"Please let me finish, or I'm afraid I'll lose my nerve."

Bronte remained quiet for him to continue.

"I've been able to light a wood burner since I was about twelve."

"Then why did you ask me . . ."

"Shush! It was an excuse to talk to you."

"Oh."

"It's you I want, Bronte. Since the first time I saw you, it's been you. I don't have a grand country estate. I don't have millions in the bank, and even if I did, I'd have no desire to spend them on polo ponies and fancy balls. I don't have an extravagant car or a second home in London, and the only 'clubs' I've ever belonged to were at university and I'm afraid they all let women wear trousers. I don't even own any fancy clothes: I hired my tux the other evening."

He stood and got down on his knees in front of Bronte. He took her hands in his, "But I am mad about you.

Absolutely one hundred per cent besotted. Have been for a long time, in fact. I can't promise to be able to change enough to make me what you want, but I can promise to spend the rest of my life trying. If you'll let me."

He continued without pause for breath, "I know Sebastian's this rich lord, but I also know you, Bronte, I know you so well, and I don't think he'll make you happy. Not really. Not forever, and not like I could. When I saw you kissing him at the ball I decided to give up. I thought I was beaten, but Camille convinced me to tell you how I feel. So basically if this all goes horribly wrong, I'm going to be blaming her."

"Camille convinced you? But she can't have, she really likes you herself! She's my best friend, she'll be devastated. I can't do that to her!"

"Camille's not interested in me."

"Ryan, I saw you two together at the ball."

"Of course you saw Camille and me together at the ball. We went together!"

"No, I saw you . . . embracing. I'd been outside with Sebastian, finishing things with him. I came in, to find you, and you and Camille were . . ."

"She was hugging me. I'd just seen you and Sebastian kissing outside and I was upset, she gave me a friendly hug to make me feel better."

"But haven't you been staying with her? I assumed that's where you'd been."

"No! I left the party and went home to see my parents. I thought it would be a good idea to put a bit of distance between us. But it didn't help. I did speak to Camille on the telephone though, and she persuaded me to give it one last shot."

"Wow," said Bronte. There was so much to process. Her heart beat faster as she absorbed his words; did he truly love her, too? The unreal dreamlike feeling of the carriage ride engulfed her again. Could she actually be this lucky?

"Did you really finish with Sebastian?" Ryan asked tentatively.

"Yes, I did. He kissed me on the terrace, and it should have been so perfect: the moonlight, the beautiful house in the background, but . . . something wasn't right. I couldn't stop thinking about you. So I left him. To be honest, I don't think I was ever with 'him'. I think I was dating my own unsatisfying fantasy."

Bronte paused then said, "But I'm sure you're wrong about Camille: are you seriously telling me you haven't noticed how attracted she is to you?"

"Um . . . that's only because she was pretending to be."

"Sorry?"

"I wanted to make you jealous," said Ryan, looking shamefaced. "You didn't seem to notice me, and Camille suggested that perhaps a little bit of healthy competition might make you more inclined to take note of some of my, I quote, 'attributes.'"

Bronte laughed. "She didn't!"

"You're not angry?"

"Of course not. It worked, didn't it? Though if I'm being completely truthful I'd definitely noticed every single one of your very fine attributes long before tonight."

"You did a very good job of hiding it."

"I don't think I wanted to admit it to myself. I was sure Sebastian was right for me, he seemed so like all the heroes I write about in my books. The whole situation was straight out of a novel! I was . . . so silly. I tried to have a relationship with the fairy tale, not the reality. I was so blinkered; I did my best to ignore my feelings for you. Even when my own writing was showing me what I needed to do. But then they just got too strong, and I couldn't ignore them any longer."

"So you'll give us a chance? Even though I'm not hero material? I know I'll never be like Sebastian."

"I wouldn't want you to be," said Bronte immediately, "Sebastian might be some other woman's hero, but he certainly isn't mine! I'm in love with you, Ryan."

"And I love you, but are you sure I'll be enough? That I'll be exciting enough . . . compared to him?"

"Ryan, when I'm with you, everything about life is exciting to me. Simply knowing you're there makes my day better. I've been such an idiot. You're wonderful, it's just taken me a long time to stop lying to myself and admit it. Love is about realising you've finally found your missing half, the person who completes you. You're my missing half."

Bronte got off her chair and knelt down beside Ryan. She took his face in her hands and kissed him, finally doing what her heart had been telling her. Warmth seemed to spread through her. It felt amazing. It felt right, like this was what the two of them were made to do.

Ryan broke away tenderly, "Your hands are freezing," he said with a smile.

"It is pretty cold," said Bronte laughing.

"Shall we take the rest of the champagne home? We can get a fire going and get warm."

"Have you got anything to eat? All this romance is all very well, but I'm starving."

"Didn't I just say I know you? I have plenty of food in. I made chilli, the first meal we shared together."

"That sounds wonderful, but what about this stuff? The table and chairs? How are we going to get that home on the buggy?"

"I didn't think of that . . ."

They both laughed. "We'll ride back in the buggy and I'll come and get everything else tomorrow. Just grab the champagne," he said.

And with that Bronte kissed him again. Ryan was, undoubtedly, the perfect hero she'd always been searching for.

THE END

Thank you for reading this book.

If you enjoyed it please leave feedback on Amazon or Goodreads, and if there is anything we missed or you have a question about, then please get in touch. We appreciate you choosing our book.

Founded in 2014 in Shoreditch, London, we at Joffe Books pride ourselves on our history of innovative publishing. We were thrilled to be shortlisted for Independent Publisher of the Year at the British Book Awards.

www.joffebooks.com

We're very grateful to eagle-eyed readers who take the time to contact us. Please send any errors you find to corrections@joffebooks.com. We'll get them fixed ASAP.